# MISCUE

## Glen Allison

YOKE
PRESS

United States of America

Cover design:  Marie Owen

Printed in the United States of America

ISBN  0-9718105-0-8


Library of  Congress Control Number 2002101105

*To Kathy,*

*who deserves more than me,*

*yet shows me*

*the simple astounding power*

*of her love daily*

# *Acknowledgements*

My thanks go to the many people who made this book possible, including my editor Carolyn Schreiter; my "first readers" Anna Fortner, Rusty & Ann Benson, Cindy Ballard, Bonnie Porter, Sandra Hendrix, Shirley King, and Randall Murphree; my encouragers Jonathan and Ashley McIntosh, Julie Homan, Malone Newell, Reesie Bradbury, Lee Jones, Jan Cooper, Kenneth Benson, Jamie Finley, Dina Plunket, Peggy Carlton Jones, Barbara Kinsey, Denny Gordon, and Ellen Aregood; and my proofers, The Sisters: Christy Grissom, Rachel Luttrell, and Darlene Donaldson.

# Prologue

*Saturday, 12:30 a.m.*

He held the scalpel above his head and twisted it slowly in the air beneath the naked light bulb. His rubber gloves blocked the chill of its metal handle. The blade caught a sharp glint of light from the bulb in the ceiling.

It would do.

He screwed the plastic cap over the blade tip and placed it on the thin bedspread.

Six-and-a-half hours until the clinic opened.

A tugboat on the distant river gave a low moan. He listened for a moment then turned to examine a selection of CDs in the small bookshelf next to the bed. The bookshelf creaked as he selected a disc and pulled it free. "The Moldau" by Smetana. He inserted the silver disc into a CD player that sat next to a Bible on the bookshelf. With his eyes closed he listened to the journey of the music as it swelled then ebbed.

From the top of the dresser he took the two Velcro straps and turned back to the bed. He positioned the straps parallel four inches apart on the blanket next to the scalpel. Shirtless, he kneeled and laid his right forearm palm up across the straps. Taking the scalpel in his left hand he held it length-wise along the inside of his forearm with the capped tip toward the inside of his elbow. He felt the cold instrument on his skin.

Bringing the straps over the arm, he tightened them to hold the scalpel secure. He flexed to test the straps, making the muscles of his forearm ripple. He rose from his kneeling position and stepped up to the mirror mounted on the wall above the dresser. With some tissue he wiped the grime from between the cracks on the glass. He stepped back and bent slightly to examine himself in the mirror before opening the top dresser drawer and taking out the green scrubs he would wear to the clinic. He pulled the top of the scrubs over his head, shook his long black hair free from beneath the collar of the cotton top, then checked his image again. The sleeve covered the scalpel well.

As he had done dozens of times, he practiced the movement of pulling up the sleeve and plucking loose the knife with his left hand. It was fluid and quick, as it would need to be.

He repeated the process several more times. Satisfied, he laid the scalpel and the straps on the bed and switched off the light. He lowered himself into the straight-backed chair by the window. Neon-tinged night and the echoes of sirens seeped through the gaps in the window frame of the old apartment. He checked his breathing. Calm. Steady.

He closed his eyes and listened to the strains of "The Moldau" as it faded away. He was long past thinking it was murder. It was justified. He was an instrument of justice. Just as a scalpel creates pain in order to bring healing. It was the right thing to do.

He sat and waited for the light.

# Chapter 1

Al Forte took one last drag from his fifth and final Checkers of the day and blew the smoke over the wrought-iron balcony rail. The exhaled puff of white drifted out past the point where his black boots were propped on the rail and faded into the late April night.

It was a bad habit and he knew it. Even if Verna hadn't harped on him about it for the past three years. He had started smoking in rehab and knew, even back then, that he would eventually quit. That's why he still smoked the vile Checkers brand. It would make giving them up easier. At least that was his story and he was sticking to it. He had gradually cut his intake down from two packs a day to one pack then down to a dozen cigarettes. Now he allowed himself a strict five per day: one upon rising, one with morning coffee, one after lunch, one after dinner, and one to cap the evening.

It was a bad habit and no excuse for it. But he'd had worse.

A black cat tightroped its way along the rail of the balcony toward Forte's feet. The cat stopped at the man's ankles where they were crossed on the rail.

"Not moving 'em, Boo," the man said. The cat looked at him when he spoke. The animal's eyes were almost the same color yellow as Forte's but looked brighter against its black background of fur. The cat stepped over the man's boots with casual care and continued his stroll along the balcony rail.

Forte's third-floor balcony was several blocks from Bourbon Street, a distance that usually separated him from the noise. This was a weekend night, however, and he could pick up snatches of noise from where he sat. He imagined a klatch of tipsy conventioneers from Iowa pausing on the corner of Bourbon and Toulouse to watch the frenzied tapping of the Peabody brothers or swaying to the offerings of a street jazzist. The music and laughter floated through the narrow streets and found him, teasing his ears. Especially the laughter of women. Somehow, of all the sweet cacophony that spilled out of the narrow east-west divider that sliced the Quarter in half, it was the high laughter of a woman that had the best chance of reaching his balcony through the muggy night.

Then again, maybe it was all just his imagination.

He smiled to himself in the dark, then sighed and stretched his arms above his head as he balanced in the tipped-back chair, feeling the muscles in his back and arms lengthen and contract. He reached over and ground out the cigarette butt into the misshapen clay ashtray on the table next to his chair. Forte stood up and stretched again. Just 15 minutes until his meeting. Enough time to walk to it.

He stepped into his dark apartment from the balcony. From a small table inside the door he retrieved a Glock nine-millimeter automatic and stuck it into a holster at the small of his back. He then picked up a lightweight leather jacket from the back of a chair and walked through the length of the apartment into the back bedroom. He stepped into the closet, locked it behind him and pressed his thumb into a tiny scanner practically unseen where it was mounted on the wall inside the closet door.

The back wall of the closet was immediately transformed into a sliding door which silently closed exactly five seconds after he stepped through it. He moved through a pitch black passageway, turned right and by memory paused after a dozen steps. Mounted about seven feet high on the wall in the darkness was another thumbprint ID scanner. Standing on tiptoe he activated it. Another hidden door slid open after a five-second delay during which a flashing green light had alerted the security guard on duty that Forte was entering the area. If he had been an intruder the flashing light would have been red and accompanied by an alarm after which all doors in the structure would have automatically locked down.

He stepped onto a catwalk that looked down on a courtyard 20 feet below. The corridor where he stood was hidden from the courtyard by one-way screens. At the far corner of the catwalk a man sat at a console of six monitors which alternately flashed the video images that were being captured by 18 cameras mounted throughout the interior and exterior of the building.

From the outside, the building looked like many others scattered throughout the Quarter: a block-long row of connected townhouses of 19th-century vintage. Forte's apartment framed one end of the building and the offices of Forte Security occupied the other end of the block. In between, however, the façade of the old building was a masquerade for what the <u>Times-Picayune</u> had called "the safest place in the world for children in danger."

It was called, simply, The Refuge. Forte had allowed a reporter and a photographer into the shelter when it was opened three years previously on the condition that he approve the article's content for security purposes. He wanted the word put out about the round-the-clock surveillance and the firepower provided by ex-Special Forces personnel. But he also wanted to ensure that the exact layout and other secrets of the shelter remained just that – secret.

This was the place, the feature article had said, "where up to a half-dozen of the most threatened children in the world could sleep soundly and play peacefully in the small playground in the courtyard.

Children who were to be witnesses against killers. Children of deposed (or deceased) rulers in lands where death now reigned. Children of celebrities who had somehow earned a spot on some serial criminal's sick list. This was a place of safety reserved for children who found themselves in a hell they didn't deserve and usually didn't understand. For a few days or weeks or sometimes months, this was a place where those children could rest easy until the cloud of danger passed – one way or another."

The article had been a little dramatic, Forte had thought at the time of publication. Three years later, he no longer thought so.

Ironically, Forte never considered himself much of a "kid" person, at least overtly. He didn't detest them; he just didn't adore having them around that much. Not like Ruth had. In a way, The Refuge had been her idea, even though Forte had planned it and made it come to life. At the time, he felt it was something he could do. Now he knew it was part of his recovery.

Forte walked toward the guard at the security console.

"All quiet, Sammy?" he asked.

"So far, chief," the man answered, his eyes still on the monitors. He idly reached up to adjust the shoulder-strap of his bullet-proof vest. "Everyone's lights were out by 11."

Forte's eyes scanned the monitors. "You heard that the drug dealers want to come get the girl? They think they can protect her from the Colombians better than we can."

The guard glanced up at Forte. "Yeah, we were briefed on that. We're double-timing our rounds over the weekend."

Forte patted him on the shoulder and walked down to the far end of the catwalk. Ahead lay another series of secret passageways which he traversed to find himself in the darkened offices of Forte Security. He walked through his office and went down the stairwell and out the entrance onto the street. Choosing to avoid Bourbon Street, he strolled down to Canal and headed toward the river. His meeting was in the Warehouse Arts District. Keeping an eye out for anything that seemed out of place, he turned right on Magazine and kept walking.

Away from the Quarter, New Orleans was like most American cities: a business district seasoned with clusters of low-income housing and run-down warehouses and infused with the homeless. The Warehouse Arts District occupied a relatively recent section of urban renewal near the river. Artists, craftspeople, antique dealers and other retailers had set up shops and studios in the re-done manufacturing plants and warehouses. The meeting had been scheduled to be held in a small upstairs gallery in the area past Julia Street.

Though the hour was late, a few couples in evening clothes were window-shopping at the funky storefronts along the route Forte had taken. Ahead of him he could see a bag lady shuffling slowly across the entrance of the alley near the gallery where the meeting was scheduled. Forte crossed Julia Street and turned the last corner to approach the staircase leading to the upstairs gallery.

He slowed his pace. Three men lolled at the bottom of the stairs. The smallest of the trio sat on the stoop while the other two leaned against the stair rails. They didn't look like they were there for the meeting.

Forte stopped ten feet away from the men.

"Evening, Poochie," he said. The small man continued to sit quietly with his elbows propped on the stairs behind him.

The two bodyguards straightened up and moved to each side of the staircase like cats stalking a bird. The man on the left wore a black leather skull cap over a shaved black head. He glanced at the small man on the steps. The bodyguard's voice sounded tortured as it rumbled deep in his throat.

"Damn, Poochie, he don't look like no SEAL." He turned back at Forte and showed white teeth in the dim light of the alley. "Looks more like a little weasel with them yellow eyes."

His partner, the lean man on the right, tugged at his rust-colored goatee and chuckled softly but kept his eyes alert.

The seated man shifted slightly and leaned forward. "Uh oh," he said. His tone was amused, however, and he didn't budge from his seated position on the stairs. The bag lady had stopped and retreated 20 yards where she watched from the alley. A middle-aged couple in tux and gown hurried around Forte with their heads lowered. They reached the street at the end of the alley before glancing back. They disappeared around the corner.

Forte slowly took three steps toward the staircase. He looked at Skull Cap. "Your mama would be ashamed of you for picking on people smaller than you, you know that?"

Skull Cap stopped smiling and looked hard at Forte. The silent one on the right took a half-step sideways and crouched slightly. Forte took in the man's movements. He would be the more dangerous of the pair.

The man sitting on the stairs casually brushed a speck from the lapel of his cashmere jacket and peered up at the sky that peeked from between the buildings. His voice was light-hearted and high-pitched. "Alvin, Alvin. Why don't we just relax and go have us a little party? You know I got your dream right here in my pocket." Poochie's smile spread across Octoroon features. "Then we can go pick up the girl."

Forte shook his head without taking his attention away from the two thugs on each side of the staircase. "Not going to happen. Kyra is safe. No one can get to her."

The smile vanished from the other man's face. "You are tough, Forte. I know that. But you don't know those people, the

Colombians." A flash of pleading crossed his face then disappeared. "They ain't civilized. They don't care who goes down."

Forte sighed. The man on the stairs had sown death in the form of white powder and magic rocks for years. Yet he could shed tears of grief over a murdered brother and could feel compassion for the fate of his tiny niece. Fearfully and wonderfully made. "Go home, Poochie. It'll be okay."

The small man held his gaze for a long moment. Finally he stood and jerked his head toward his bodyguards. Skull Cap did not break his glare for a long moment then followed his boss. Goatee trailed after them. Poochie walked to the end of the alley, stopped and lit a cigar. He called out to Forte.. "This time we came just to talk." His voice had lost its lightness. In the flame of the match, his eyes looked flat. "Next time…" He dropped the match as he turned and walked out of the alley.

Forte watched him go. He looked up at the gallery window at the top of the stairs. Several heads were looking down at him. He went up the stairs and into the gallery. About two dozen chairs were arranged in four rows. He recognized some of the people: casino workers, a couple of waitresses from clubs in the Quarter, an off-duty cop, a lawyer, a dock worker, a Tulane professor, a hooker. He took a chair on the back row and caught the eye of Manning Laird on the other end of the row. Manny's leathery face twisted into the closest thing to a smile he could conjure. Forte leaned back and relaxed.

A bespectacled man in a rumpled suit had just walked up to a podium at the front of the room and cleared his throat. He looked like someone's low-rent bookkeeper. The man pushed his glasses up on his nose.

"Hello," he said. "My name is Jimmy and I'm an addict."

# Chapter 2

*Saturday, 7:30 a.m.*

Dr. Tyson Lamberth guided his Lexus past the protestors and into the guarded parking lot under the clinic. He carefully looked through all the windows of the vehicle before stepping out of the car. Even though he had taken a random route to his office, different from the one he'd taken the day before and the day before that, he knew it always paid to exercise caution these days. The crazies were still out there, he reminded himself.

He always arrived early on Saturday. It was his busiest day of the week, and he was looking forward to it. Not only was it a beautiful spring morning, it was his birthday. Even the misguided souls on the sidewalk out front would not put a dent in his good mood today. His sailboat was at the dock, ready to take him away at the end of the day.

The doctor greeted the security guard at the elevator as he hummed the Beatles tune he'd been listening to on the car's CD player. *What was the name of that one … Ah, yes, "Here Comes the Sun."* Today he turned 40. He had been three years old when The Fab Four had arrived in America at JFK Airport. As a child he was playing little league out in Metairie when the group broke up. But

then again, when had their music ever been out of style? *Little darlin',
it's been a long cold lonely winter.* The elevator door parted and he strolled
down the corridor to his office.

Gleaming stainless steel and white tile was everywhere.
Everything in his clinic was spotless and state-of-the art. He made
sure of it from the start when he had personally supervised its
construction. The leather sofas in the waiting room, the networked
computers in the reception area and throughout the building, the
latest advancements in sonogram videography and procedures —
everything about the Lamberth Center spoke of excellence and
competence. His patients deserved it. And more important, *HE*
deserved it.

As he passed the lobby area, he saw a tall figure bending over to
empty a garbage can. The man's back was to the doctor but
Lamberth could see the man's dark hair banded into a pony tail. It
was the clinic's disposal technician. The doctor greeted him
"Morning, Brent" before going into his office. Once seated at his
desk he called up the day's schedule on his computer. The first
procedure was scheduled for 8:00 a.m. and would call for the extra
equipment in Procedure Room A at the other end of the clinic. He
reached over and slightly rearranged the photo of his wife and
daughter on the otherwise empty desktop. Mustn't keep happiness
waiting. *Here comes the sun. It's all right.*

In the prep room he donned his scrubs and stood at the sink
scrubbing his hands. His patients deserved the sterile atmosphere his
clinic offered. No back-alley butcher room here. The mirror above
the sink had been mounted extra high so he would not have to stoop
to see himself. He reached up to push an errant lock of brown hair
back under the surgical cap, then leaned close to the mirror. The fine
wrinkles at the corners of his light brown eyes only enhanced his
good looks, women had confided in him. "You magnificent bastard,"
he told his mirror image.

The male operating room nurse came through the door and pulled on rubber gloves. He already had scrubbed in and had donned a surgical mask and cap. He knew the doctor's insistence on a sterile environment. He picked up the doctor's gloves and handed them to him, then carefully placed the doctor's glasses on his face. Lamberth smiled vaguely but took little notice of his helper. "Thanks, David," he mumbled. He was entering "The Zone," as he called it. The Zone was a near-euphoric feeling that engulfed him just before a procedure such as this one. His assistants knew to remain silent unless he asked a direct question.

He moved into the procedure room where his patient was in position with her feet in stirrups. The surgical blanket that stretched across her knees was designed to block her view of the small table beneath her legs. Tyson moved to her side and gently stroked her forehead. "Joyce, I'm Dr. Lamberth and I'm going to take care of you." He made eye contact with her, his eyes friendly above the mask, then moved around the table and resumed his humming. *Here comes the sun. Here comes the sun.*

The woman, a divorced stockbroker with a 13-year-old daughter, had startled at his touch before giving him a weak smile. She was grateful that the clinic had been able to schedule her so quickly. The breakup with her fiancé had come out of the blue. For six months the couple had talked about how it would be, how they would raise the new baby together. Now he was gone and she was left to make the right decision. It wasn't fair, she thought, but when had life been fair? It was a struggle enough to keep Angie away from drugs and boys and… And everything else destructive that seemed to swirl around teenagers these days. Neither Angie nor the newborn would have gotten the attention they deserved. This was the best thing to do. Besides, deep down, Joyce knew that a mid-30's woman with two children stood little chance of meeting someone new to share her life.

The doctor would perform a D&X procedure, for Dilate and Extract. The anti-abortion nuts called it a partial birth abortion. Lamberth thought of the procedure in more clinical terms. The woman's cervix is dilated, and the fetus is partially removed from the womb, feet first. The surgeon inserts a sharp object into the back of the fetus' head to create a small opening into which he inserts a vacuum tube through which the brains are extracted. The head of the fetus contracts at this point and allows the fetus to be more easily removed from the womb.

He had performed hundreds of D&X's, some even in the third trimester. Dozens of women's lives had been saved by the procedure, he believed. He had seen patients who would have surely suffered physically and emotionally from a continued pregnancy. He knew that many of the fetuses, if they had been delivered alive, never would have gained consciousness or ,worse, would have died shortly after birth from hydrocephalus.

He held out his hand for the forceps, which his assistant gave him. Bending slightly, he lifted the edge of Joyce's gown and inserted the instrument. Applying steady pressure, he opened the forceps and began to induce the breech delivery.

His feeling of well-being had risen to the point that he imagined this was what drug addicts experienced. He had campaigned for women's rights since his days in medical school and felt genuinely thankful that he could make such a difference in women's lives. In his heart of hearts he considered himself a liberator. He had never shared that conviction with anyone else, but he felt called to his life as one was called to a  mission. A mission of bringing freedom. Because of him, his patients were free from archaic practices and a ridiculous moral code. He had shared his gift with several girlfriends over the years, and even with his wife so she could devote herself to making a home for their daughter. *Here comes the sun. Here comes the sun. And I say, it's all right.*

Now he was giving this gift to Joyce.

Reaching under the gown, he gently probed her abdomen to determine the placement of the head of the fetus. "Just relax," he said soothingly. Pushing and guiding, he moved the fetus so that first one foot then the other appeared at the opening. Tugging gently, he slid out the small form until the legs, torso and arms appeared. He stopped so that the head of the fetus was still inside the woman.

Everything was still now. It always seemed like a dream to him, but not an unpleasant one. Now for the next step. Time for the instrument to create the opening at the base of the fetus' skull to insert the vacuum tube. The body of the fetus was supported in a small sling connected to a crossbar between the stirrups. He held it steady with his left hand and held out his right hand palm up.

"Trachon," he ordered.

The doctor kept his head down. He heard a rustling noise. What was that sound... Velcro? But... no trachon. Nothing happened.

Dr. Lamberth glanced up from his hands to look sharply at his assistant's masked face. "Trachon!" He insisted on 100 percent efficiency in his clinic.

He looked down at his helper's hands. His brow furrowed. "Not a scalpel, you idiot. The incision would be too small for..."

The doctor looked up into the blue eyes of his helper.

But today David's eyes were brown.

The doctor's brow furrowed, puzzled. Then he understood.

Time froze and the room emptied of all sound.

The woman's voice broke the deathly quiet. "What is going..." She had tilted her head forward. She gasped and clutched at her stomach. "Oh no..."

She heard a gurgling noise, then felt something heavy slump against her leg and thud to the floor.

Then another voice. A calm voice.

"Lie still, ma'am, and close your eyes. I want you to push. Now."

The woman gasped.

More silence. Then a baby's squeal.

She felt a pressure on her chest and looked down.

The tiny newborn squirmed. And screamed.

Suddenly she heard another scream, even louder than the baby's.

She realized it was hers.

# Chapter 3

*Saturday, 10:30 a.m.*

Forte leaned back in the chair and kept very still. He could think of only a handful of people he would trust to hold a razor against his neck. Larue Hebert was on the short list. Near the top.

He closed his eyes and breathed in the essence of the old barber shop as the man shuffled around to shave the other side of his face. The place smelled the same as it had when he first roller-skated off the brick street and through the door almost 30 years ago at age seven. Hair oil, cracked leather chairs, and freshly laundered towels. The small shop with its three barber chairs smelled clean and looked orderly. "Cost about nuttin' to be clean, cher" Larue had intoned in his quiet Creole accent countless times in Forte's hearing. The barber shop on Felicity Street was spotless if worn. Al knew that fact from experience; he'd swept up enough hair from the tiled floor to weave a carpet for the SuperDome.

"And the man Poochie, he just sit there, him?" Larue leaned forward to guide the razor under Al's neck.

"He seemed to enjoy the show," Forte said.

"But le fillette, he want her back, huh?"

"He thinks he can protect her better." Forte opened his eyes and studied the fluorescent lights hanging from the stained ceiling. "Mostly he's scared for her. He doesn't know how to show it except with a threat of violence."

The rhythmic scraping of the razor was mixed with the white noise of the TV set on the wall. "And you show him some trouble back, eh." The old man's voice was quieter, almost as if he were talking to himself.

Forte shifted his gaze and refocused his eyes to study the man's café au lait features as he continued shaving him. Larue's face was expressionless as always.

"Not this time, Rue. It was just a little dance. Not the full mardi gras."

The barber silently busied himself wiping the excess hot lather off the younger man's face before he turned and retrieved an electric razor from the counter behind him. He snapped on the No. 2 tool and clicked it on. The buzz of the razor preempted further conversation and drowned out the television. As the barber ran the clippers over his head, Forte let his eyes sweep over the familiar framed items on the wall above the mirror opposite his chair.

A framed newspaper clipping and photo of Forte slam-tackling Lucky Battier in the 1981 Holy Cross-Jesuit High game. A picture of Al and the hulking Mack Quadrie in graduation gowns clowning it up while Larue stood by with hands folded solemnly in front of him. A photo of his Navy ceremony. The picture of Al, Ruth, and Larue in wedding garb in front of St. Louis Cathedral. The article about the opening of The Refuge. A photo of Forte's grandmother with her dazzling smile framed by a 50's beehive. A photo of Larue's beautiful wife taken a decade before the cancer claimed her.

The clippers went silent just as a burst of noise erupted from the barber chair next to Forte's.

"You don't stop that squirming I'm gonna snatch you baldheaded before Bebo can cut your hair." A woman in a waitress uniform lounged in one of the waiting chairs and pointed a thick black finger at the other barber chair. In the chair, a small head poked above the snap-on gown that covered his entire body and hung a foot past his toes. The boy froze and rolled his eyes toward the only other barber in the shop. Bebo, the barber, looked down at the boy and nodded. He rubbed a hand over his own slick ebony head. "That's what happened to me wayyyy back when I was your age. Mmm hmm, shonuff. One minute I had a head full o' hair. Next minute, whoosh, slick as a bowling ball. Mmm hmm."

Forte winked at the boy. The boy's eyebrows rose but the rest of his face remained still.

On the television screen a photo of a man's face appeared. Bebo picked up the remote and turned up the volume. "This is what I told you about. Listen."

The television screen showed a woman holding a microphone, standing in front of a police barricade around a modern-looking building. "It was here that Dr. Tyson Lamberth was murdered this morning while performing an operation. Police say he was stabbed at the base of his skull by an unknown assailant using a sharp object. The murderer then fled the clinic on foot. Lamberth, a nationally-recognized proponent of women's reproductive rights, had received death threats recently but police say they have no leads yet on the identity of his murderer."

Behind the reporter a group of protestors gestured at the TV cameras. A man thrust a sign with the words "Baby Killer" splashed in red paint. Another man grabbed the sign and the pair started grappling as the news report transitioned to another story.

Bebo turned down the sound with the remote. "Rich white folks killing each other." He winced and looked at Al. "No offense, Alvin."

Forte could feel the tickle of Larue's brush as it slapped the black hairs off the back of his neck. "No problem, Bebo. I'm not that rich really."

The bald barber grinned. The phone rang and he picked it up and answered it. "Yes, he's here." He handed the phone to Forte. "It's Verna."

To say Verna Griffey was his housekeeper or assistant always seemed like a laughable understatement to Forte. New clients visiting Forte Security were likely to be confronted with her hulking African-American form blocking the entrance to the interior offices if they showed up unannounced. But she had been a friend of Al and Ruth's long before The Refuge had opened. Now she and her ex-cop husband Archie took care of practically all the details in his life, from cleaning his apartment to answering his e-mail when he was out of town. He had not asked for the help. It just seemed to work out, and now the Griffeys were on the payroll of Forte Security. He picked up the phone and spoke briefly. He listened for a moment then hung up.

The barber shop was quiet now except for the drone of the television. Larue had stopped sweeping the floor and Bebo stood with his clippers poised above the boy's head. The boy's mother peeked over the top of a Cosmopolitan magazine that displayed a waif of a model on the cover.

Forte took his jacket from the coat rack in the corner. He looked around at everyone. "So I'm supposed to give you an update now?" Everyone – Larue, Bebo, the boy, and his mother – kept looking at him. "Okay. Verna got a call at the office from Dr. Lamberth's wife. His widow, I guess I should say. She wants protection for their 11-year-old daughter." He shrugged into the jacket. "Now you have the latest update on my business. Happy?"

Bebo nodded, serious. "Hell, Alvin. You know we ain't got no lives around here. We gotta borrow some excitement any ways we can."

Forte shook his head, smiled, and looked down at Larue. They shook hands. "Thanks, Rue."

The old man tilted his face down slightly, still expressionless. "Take care, cher."

Forte smiled. "I'll take as much as I can get."

# Chapter 4

Studying his dark eyes and long black hair in the mirror, the killer decided he definitely would not miss this look. It had served his purposes, but six months was long enough.

That's what the TV news had called him. The killer. The murderer. He had expected as much. But what would the hundreds, maybe thousands, of children say, those whose lives would be spared because of him? What would they call him?

Of course, they would never know, he mused as he bent over the bathroom sink. He cupped his hand under his left eye and blinked hard. A brown-colored contact lens dropped from his eye into his hand. He repeated the process on his right eye. He straightened up, blinked again and looked into the mirror at his ice-blue eyes. Their natural color. Much better.

The small rented house overlooked a quiet street in a respectable section of Gretna across the river from New Orleans. He had leased it months earlier and had stocked it with provisions and clothes during a couple of midnight trips. Everything had been bought from Wal-Mart stores in sleepy coastal towns like Waveland and Pass Christian across the state line in Mississippi. Under cover of night, he had unloaded the goods from his van to the back door of the small house from the driveway that wound around to the back of the building. No one in the neighborhood had seen him. But even if someone had, he would have seen a man in a long blond ponytail with a Fu Manchu moustache.

After he had finished his business at the clinic, he had driven north across Lake Pontchartrain on the causeway, away from the river, in the old blue Pinto he had borrowed from his co-worker after taping the man's mouth shut with duct tape and leaving him otherwise unharmed. After about 40 minutes of driving, he had stopped and bought gas deliberately with his Brent Garrison credit card. He then went directly to the bus station in a nearby town and tossed the credit card under one of the scarred wooden benches in the waiting area. He drove away from the bus station for a few more miles then guided the rickety car through increasingly smaller backroads until he reached the abandoned shack. No one had noticed the shiny new padlock on the creaking wooden doors of the shack. He had unlocked it, backed the van out and pulled the Pinto into the building and relocked the doors. He had driven the van back through New Orleans then taken the Huey Long Bridge across the Mississippi River and meandered his way to the house in Gretna. It had been risky but necessary. He wanted the police looking for a north-bound Pinto traveling toward Arkansas.

He had nearly reached the last leg of a journey that had been a year and a half in the making. He had carefully made his contacts through an anonymous Internet chat room. He had searched for the new identity for months before finding the right one. A social security card was obtained, after which came a drivers license, library card, credit cards. Then another wait until the job at the clinic had come open. And finally the six grueling months at the clinic.

The work at the clinic wasn't tough physically. Just emptying the garbage, buffing the floors, vacuuming the carpet. It was the disposal of the remains that got him. The doctors and their assistants referred to it as "fetal tissue" that invariably was picked up by medical couriers and taken to research labs.

He forced himself to think of it as "remains."

After a half-year of seeing the process close at hand, he knew he had made the right decision to begin with. Unlike Reverend Paul Hill in Pensacola, however, he never planned to hang around and be made a martyr. He had studied Hill's writings and watched the TV interviews with Ted Koppel and others that Hill had conducted before the pastor had blasted an abortion doctor with a shotgun on July 29, 1994. He agreed with Hill's writing to the core, which argued that lethal force was justifiable in the defense of an unborn child. He just thought the good reverend had not planned the actual operation very thoroughly.

First, Hill had also accidentally killed the escort who had been sitting in the car next to the abortion doctor. That victim was ill-advised in his choice of professions at the particular moment. But he did not deserve to die. Second, Hill had not waited until the doctor was actually poised to kill an unborn child. In that exact instant, deadly force was justified to defend the child against an attacker, just as if a murderer had burst into a home trying to stab to death a one-day-old baby. What man would not kill the murderous attacker of a child if it meant saving a baby's life?

He knew, however, that no court of law would see it his way. Therefore, he had been more careful in this operation. Death row wasn't for him. He had more work to do.

He walked out of the bathroom and to the hall closet to retrieve a bed sheet. The television in the den was tuned to a news station. He stopped as an update appeared on the screen. "A prime suspect has been identified in the murder of New Orleans doctor Tyson Lamberth, according to an FBI spokesperson," the woman newscaster intoned. "Police are searching for Brent Garrison, an employee at the Lamberth Clinic who was last seen at the clinic early this morning before the doctor was murdered." A grainy photo taken from Garrison's ID photo flashed on the screen. Dark eyes, black hair, brooding mouth. His "Brent Garrison" identity had worked exactly as he planned.

The news said nothing about the baby he had saved. He wondered what became of it. The killer listened to the TV news for a moment longer then returned to the bathroom.

He spread the bed sheet on the floor under the sink. Out of the cabinet he took scissors, electric hair clippers, a comb and a bottle of bleach. He set them on the narrow glass shelf above the sink. He took the scissors in his left hand and stood up to face himself in the mirror.

Pulling a long strand of black away from his head, he clipped it an inch away from his skull. He dropped the lock of hair on the floor.

He smiled. Coming back to normal. This would be better. Much better.

# Chapter 5

*Saturday, noon.*

The Lamberth home probably wasn't the biggest in the Garden District. Forte guessed that it was in the running.

He stood in the kitchen drinking coffee with a city cop. Catered deli meats, cheeses, and pastries filled the counters on all sides of them. It could have been preparations for a party except for the stricken faces of the servants and the police cars lining the winding driveway outside the kitchen window. A maid came into the kitchen with a silver coffee pot. Forte waved her off but the cop held up his heavy porcelain cup for a refill. "Gracias, Maria." The maid nodded and walked into the next room.

The cop faced the window as he drank. "Guess his kind of work brought in the big bucks," he said. His voice was flat with a thin edge of disgust.

"You know what kind of work he did?" Forte said.

"Yeah."

"You don't like it?"

"Not my job to like it or not like it."

"Yeah. But you've got your opinions."

The cop looked at him. "Yup. I got opinions. Lots of 'em." He set his cup on the counter top. "But my opinions, they ain't about to come out and dance around here today." He gave an almost imperceptible jerk of his head toward the dining room. The mayor, a councilwoman, and the district attorney grazed at a gargantuan food-laden table as they waited to pay their respects.

The three at the table looked up expectantly as a man in a butler's outfit scurried past them and came into the kitchen. He addressed Forte. "Mrs. Lamberth will see you now." Forte followed the butler through a maze of hallways that finally ended in a small parlor overlooking a garden. The curved bank of windows in the room ran from the floor to the ceiling. Outside, a bumblebee darted up to the center window and hovered there, then sped off among the sunlit splashes of flowers in the garden.

A woman stood at the window, her arms crossed over her chest with her back to the room. A barrel-chested man wearing a scowl was sitting on a loveseat against the wall. The butler backed out of the room, closing the French doors behind him.

"Thank you for coming, Mr. Forte. Please have a seat," the woman said without turning around. Her voice was deep. Any other day, it might have been called sultry. Today it came out with a hoarseness bordering on tears. She lowered her head and her properly tangled hair looked copper as it caught the sunlight in the window. Slowly she turned and walked to a chair next to the loveseat, looking as if an abrupt movement might shatter her. "I'm Freida Lamberth, Mr. Forte." She brushed a lock of hair away from emerald eyes now rimmed in red. "And this is Mr. Tolan. He is helping with some of the…with some of the details today." She gestured with a slim, firm arm that seemed to operate on its own, as if she were guessing what a normal movement would look like. She dropped her hand back into her lap. The scowling man made eye contact with Forte and nodded once.

She looked at neither of the men as she spoke, her eyes focused at a spot somewhere out in the garden beyond the windows. "Mr. Forte, you know about the murder of my husband." Her eyes brimmed full.

"Yes. I'm sorry for your loss."

She nodded, tilted her head up, then lowered it again. She blinked twice slowly. A long moment of silence filled the room. "Thank you," the woman said.

Forte waited. When death visited a home, time itself became malleable – shrinking then stretching, sometimes within the same few moments of a conversation or in the middle of some simple task. He had seen it before. He had lived through it before.

She coughed once and her voice was clearer now. "I want you to protect my daughter. Until they catch whoever…" Her shoulders rose as she inhaled deeply. "…whoever did this. I know you specialize in cases such as these. I remember the incident with the Christenberry boy."

"Yes, we were fortunate to recover him so quickly," said Forte. The case had gained national attention a couple of years past and had established Forte Security's reputation in child kidnapping cases. Two men in Italy had paid with their lives for the mistake of calling his bluff in a stand-off.

Freida turned to look at him directly. He could see tiny freckles sprinkled across her cheeks, which were shiny with tears now. "Can you keep Hallee safe, Mr. Forte?"

He had heard the tone in her voice dozens of times. More than pleading, it was the terrified grasping for any solid emotional handhold on a tear-slick cliff of grief. Most of the time, his answer proved to be true in the long run. A few times the answer didn't turn out to be true. But at this moment, when the question was first asked, there was only one response. He always answered it the same way.

"Yes. We will," he said.

She searched his eyes for a moment, then gave the smallest of nods. "Thank you." She stood up and both men rose to their feet. "Mr. Tolan will talk with you about the details, if you don't mind. I must receive the mayor now." She held out her hand and Forte shook it. Her fingers felt strong but her grip was without conviction.

When she had left, the scowling man remained standing but waved Forte to be seated.

"Mr. Forte, I will be direct with you. We don't think you are the best one for this job. Mrs. Lamberth insisted, however, so we will cooperate with you fully."

Forte had seen men like him before, too. Probably competent but overconfident. Accustomed to commanding attention with a stern or forceful word or two. Bullies. It had been a major challenge to his military career at times when he had to deal with these types. Now it was merely a challenge to his patience. And sometimes a nuisance.

Forte smiled. "I appreciate that. Just exactly who is 'we'?"

"Pardon me?"

"You said 'We will cooperate.' Who is 'we'?"

"I'm a security consultant for the national office of the NCLU."

"Ah. The National Civil Liberties Union. And you knew Dr. Lamberth."

"Yes, he was a supporter. A big supporter."

"And you think you could have done this job better?"

"Yes, I do."

"And why is that?"

Tolan breathed deeply then exhaled. He looked at Forte then sat on the love seat again. "For one thing, we do not believe your heart will be in it."

"Why do you think that?

"May I be blunt?"

"Why change your style now?"

Tolan's face colored with anger but his voice stayed even. "We know that you grew up Catholic, even if you are not a practicing churchgoer right now. We believe you do not support the kind of work that Dr. Lamberth was doing."

"And that's it?"

Tolan paused only briefly. "Well, there's the matter of your, umm, shall we say, your period of instability."

Forte cocked his head and looked contemplative. "My 'period of instability.' I like that."

The other man frowned. "Your use of drugs. Your cocaine addiction. We know you were never arrested for it. We know you completed a drug treatment program three years ago." Tolan leaned forward and made a tent of his fingers in front of him. "Nothing personal, but we think it's a reflection of your ability, in our opinion." He paused. "Ultimately, we think it is a weakness and a flaw that could mean failure … in this case."

Forte sighed. He didn't blame the man. There was a time when he would have thought exactly the same way. "You've done your homework fast. And you shared all of this insight with Mrs. Lamberth."

"Yes, we did."

"And she chose to ignore your advice?"

Tolan broke eye contact and turned a bitter face toward the garden. "Yes."

"I wonder why she made that choice?"

The other man breathed deeply, then spoke through his teeth. "Because of your background as a Navy SEAL. Because of your reputation for protecting children."

"Mr. Tolan, tell me. Exactly what is your role here?"

"Mrs. Lamberth asked me to show you the layout of the house and explain the security system to you."

"And beyond that, do you have any official part to play in the ongoing security of Hallee Lamberth?"

Tolan's eyes had now taken on the furious look of a pitbull on a stout chain. "None. She said her attorney would sign your contract on Monday."

Forte studied the man. He had seen plenty like him: men who lived by a prescribed plan and if they were forced to deviate from that plan somehow, they became angry. Or defiant. Or both. He had been in that place himself. "Before we begin our tour of the security system, Mr. Tolan, let me say something.

"First, my job here is to keep a child safe. That's it. Any views I might have on abortion do not affect that job.

"Second, it is true I have screwed up my life in the past. I'm a recovering addict. I can choose to spend my days apologizing for that weakness. No excuse for that. I can't force you or anyone else to accept me or believe me or trust me. That's beyond my control, so I try not worry about it. I try to spend my time on things I can do something about. Or I can choose to use whatever abilities I have to do my job the best I can.

"And third." He looked over at the window again. The bee was back. From the other side of the glass it seemed to be watching him. "The third thing is just a comment. I'm a wee bit surprised that a group like the NCLU, an organization with such a well known reputation for helping the down-trodden, would be so, what's the word I want... how about... judgmental, about any person's so-called weakness." The bee zigzagged away abruptly.

A flush crept up Tolan's face from beneath his collar. His broad face kept the scowl but he held his tongue.

Forte smiled again. "That's okay." A cloud had blocked the sun for a moment. A shadow covered the flowers beyond the glass.

"Everybody makes a mistake now and then."

# Chapter 6

Police barricades and yellow "Crime Scene" tape still surrounded the Lamberth Clinic. The media vans had departed, but not before mutilating the front lawn of the clinic. Tire ruts crisscrossed the St. Augustine grass. Some plastic cups and a few torn posters littered the sidewalk that bordered the lawn. As Forte eased his motorcycle to a stop on the sidewalk, a van with Gidot Lawnscapers on the side and a trailer full of sod in tow pulled up to the curb. Two men got out of the cab and hurriedly began unloading rakes, shovels, and a large roller.

The tour of the security system at the Lamberth house had been performed efficiently by Tolan. Freida Lamberth had continued receiving condolences from a Who's Who sampling of Louisiana's leaders. Hallee, the Lamberths' 11-year-old daughter, had kept the door to her room closed but not tight enough to contain the muffled sobs coming from inside. Forte had made plans to return late in the evening for the first overnight shift. Federal marshals and city cops would keep the house safe until then. As Forte had pulled his bike away from the curb, he looked back to catch the curtains fluttering shut in the girl's second story window.

At the clinic, the New Orleans police had been relegated to securing the perimeter of the property while the FBI handled the actual investigation. A cop who looked like he could play Schwartzenegger's body double was blocking the front entrance of the clinic. As Forte approached with his helmet under one arm, the cop eyed him from behind aviator shades.

"Police investigation, sir. The clinic is closed for the day," the cop said.

"Check the list," Forte said. "Al Forte"

The cop peered at the clipboard then at Forte. "Identification?" the cop asked.

Forte flipped open his wallet to his driver's license and investigator's license. The cop waved him through the front door and the empty reception area of the clinic.

Much of the staff and the clinic's patients had been interviewed and released. Two separate FBI forensic teams were still at work. One of the teams bustled through an intersection in the hallway wearing plastic gloves and shoe-coverings held to their ankles with elastic. The clear plastic on their shoes whisked across the white-tiled floor as they disappeared around the corner. The whisking sound was not quite in tempo with the Enya tune that drifted from the speakers in the drop ceiling of the hallway.

Straight ahead a tall woman in a dark blue suit was pointing to a diagram on a clipboard lying on a countertop. A man a few inches shorter than the woman looked at the diagram and nodded. Both of them looked up as Forte approached. Their faces were professionally neutral. The woman handed the clipboard to the other man.

"Take this to the team in the garage." The man hurried away. The woman turned to face Forte.

"You must have an angel high up in Justice looking out for you," she said. "We aren't even letting the city cops in here. Yet, here you are."

"I guess the Lamberths have some pull," Forte said.

"I guess," she said. "Follow me." From the countertop, she picked up a leather-covered notebook with the FBI logo and the name "Rosalind Dent" stamped in silver on the cover. She motioned for Forte to follow her to a vacant office down the hall.

The FBI agent sat at the chair behind the desk and took a notebook out of her jacket pocket. She moved a stack of medical insurance forms from the center of the desktop to one side and placed the notebook in front of her. Without looking up, she said, "Al, I know you can be trusted most of the time. But we both know you are a cowboy. You can't color outside the lines in a case like this. I don't have to tell you how sensitive this is. This is strictly FBI and everyone in the bureau all the way up to the Attorney General will be getting daily updates."

On a fabric bulletin board behind the desk were two children's drawings, a photo of a mom and a dad and two kids, a NOW button and a dozen or so sticky notes. One of the kid's drawings was a stick-figure with a sword fighting an unrecognizable creature. In the other drawing, a figure that looked like an angel was sitting in a tree next to a blue house.

Forte set his motorcycle helmet on the corner of desktop. "You know, Rosie, that suit really does compliment your complexion. And by the way, nice to see you."

The woman looked at him hard for a moment then let her face relax. "I'm being a tough case, huh?" She pushed away from the desk, leaned back and rocked her head from side to side to stretch her neck muscles. "Lot of pressure these days. First the promotion, now this."

Forte nodded. "It will be fine. They wouldn't have made you Special Agent in Charge if you couldn't handle it. And you don't have to worry about me. I will try so hard to behave. The only reason I'm here is that Lamberth's murder might have a bearing on my current assignment."

"Protecting the Lamberth girl," she said.

"Yes. They've had threats for years. Now this. The mother is scared."

"Who wouldn't be." She waved a hand vaguely at the doorway. "The guy who did this had his act together." She flipped a page in the notebook. "Here's the scoop, as we know it so far.

"The killer was in the room with Dr. Lamberth, assisting him. The patient said she couldn't see his face because of the surgical mask. She described him as tall; she thought he had dark hair but it was covered by a surgical cap. Right before the final stage of the abortion, the assistant stabbed the doctor in the back of the neck at the base of his skull. Death was virtually instantaneous.

"The killer then delivered the child, cut the umbilical cord, put the baby on the mother's chest, then left the procedure room. The woman screamed but no one came to investigate. The doctors and nurses said an occasional scream was not unusual. No one inside the clinic noticed anything for nearly 20 minutes. Another assistant came to check the room and found the doctor dead on the floor with the scalpel stuck in his neck. The woman was out of her head.

"A couple of nurses saw the assistant walking down the hallway around the time of the murder but they didn't pay any attention to him. The guard in the parking garage saw a light blue Ford Pinto leave the garage at approximately 8:45 a.m.

"Some scrubs with blood on them were recovered from a garbage can in the garage just outside the elevators. Fingerprints from the procedure room have been lifted but we won't know if they tell us anything different for a few hours. Probably *won't* tell us anything. All employees undergo a pretty thorough security check before being hired.

"Two employees from the clinic are unaccounted for. David Butler, the assistant who was scheduled for the procedure this morning, and Brent Garrison, the disposal technician for the clinic. Both are tall and dark-haired. David Butler has worked at the clinic for two years. Brent Garrison for six months. Garrison has facial hair and Butler is smooth-faced. Neither of them is at their homes and both of their vehicles are missing. Butler drives the blue pinto. Right now, Garrison is the prime suspect.

"Whether the killer acted alone, we don't know, but based on the past attacks at clinics, we have to assume he was part of a larger conspiracy."

The FBI agent paused and absently ran her hand over the closely cropped black hair at the back of her neck. Her face was ivory and angular and free from makeup except for eye liner. The only wrinkle came from the small furrow on her forehead as she scanned her notes.

She looked across the desk at Forte. "We are treating this as a hate crime with the anti-abortion terrorist groups as prime suspects. The FBI has infiltrated some of those groups. The most recent threats have come from Jason Hamilton's group in Houston, Texas. He's the pastor who threw the pig's blood on Lamberth at that banquet last fall. From our interviews with Freida Lamberth and others, there seems to be no one else with a more recent connection."

Forte looked at his reflection in the shiny maroon finish of his helmet on the desk. The curve of the helmet gave him a Jimmy Durante look. He said nothing.

Dent studied him for a beat, then said, "Nothing to add, Al?"

"Hate crime. That term always gets me," Forte said.

"Why?" she asked.

"C'mon, Rosie. The guy's dead. Murder is murder. Why does the government have a special label for certain types of killings? As far as I'm concerned, if someone has been murdered, it's all hate."

"No, not true. Some crimes are motivated by bias against another person's beliefs. And that falls into another category."

"Motivated by bias," Forte repeated. "So, because the killer was biased against an abortion provider, that killer is put in another category. And not even bias because of race or sexual orientation or anything else. Just bias against someone he believed was killing a baby."

The woman leaned forward. "The doctor was performing a procedure that is protected by law. There has been hate rhetoric for years using the same language you just used – 'baby killing.' And that rhetoric has been linked to murders, several of them."

Forte held up his hands. "Don't paint me with a broad brush stroke." He leaned back in his chair. "Do I think abortion is right? No, I don't. Do I think these terrorists should take the law into their own hands, become vigilantes and kill all the abortion doctors? No, I don't buy that either.

"But I am tired of the government putting labels on crimes just because the government thinks those crimes were motivated by a certain type of thinking, a certain mindset that the government didn't like. That's like saying that any of us should be outlawed from thinking certain thoughts. And that's a scary concept."

The FBI agent leaned back in her chair and rubbed her eyes with the tips of her fingers. Her nails looked like they had been chewed short. "Al, I don't know why I get into these discussions with you. You know that I am closer to your viewpoint than a lot of people in my position would be. But I have a job to do. And the current law is the only one I have to work with." She closed the notebook. "By the way, the NCLU people are not happy that Mrs. Lamberth chose you to be the bodyguard for her daughter. They tried to block you from access to our investigation."

Forte picked up the helmet from the desk and studied his distorted reflection. "What about you, Rosie? You think my so-called pro-life views will affect my ability to protect the Lamberth child?"

The agent stood up. Her eyes were slightly red from the rubbing. "I think they have nothing to worry about."

Forte stood also and walked with Dent to the front door of the clinic. He lit his third Checkers of the day, took a drag and blew the smoke out toward the street. The agent grimaced slightly but said nothing. Forte started to put on his helmet, then stopped and turned back to Dent. "Almost forgot to ask. What happened to the woman and her baby?"

Dent looked puzzled. "What woman?"

"The witness. The woman who came in for the abortion but ended up with a child."

The FBI agent nodded. "She's resting at  Tulane Medical Center." She paused. "Last time we saw her she was nursing the baby and talking goo goo to her. I think she was coming out of shock. Lucky woman."

"Lucky kid," Forte said.

# Chapter 7

"UNHHH!" Forte grunted as the man's roundhouse kick caught him in the ribs. He staggered slightly then danced away from the second kick: a sweep-kick designed to take his legs out from under him. He huffed twice through his teeth and circled to his right. Gotta be quick. Gotta concentrate.

The workout room at Forte Security stayed busy a good part of the day – and night. The guards from The Refuge used it to keep in shape and break up the monotony of their duty, especially the graveyard shift. Some free-weights and a couple of bench-press benches lined one end of the room. The blue mats for hand-to-hand practice bouts occupied the rest of the room. Some Wynton Marsalis riffs wafted from the sound system in the corner.

Forte feinted with a left jab to the jaw and drove his right glove into his partner's midsection. He ducked a roundhouse punch then high-kicked twice, snapping his opponents head back with the first and putting him on the mat with the second. Wynton's horn wailed a high note. Forte bent down to give the man a hand up. They high-fived and the other man headed for the showers. Forte drained a water bottle, shucked off his gloves and head-protector, laced up his running shoes and jogged down the stairs and out onto the street.

He headed north away from the busiest part of the Quarter, crossed Rampart and stayed on Iberville alongside St. Louis Cemetery. The sun had won the afternoon battle with the clouds for the moment, bathing the above-ground tombs of New Orleans's oldest cemetery with warm light. As Forte glided past the mausoleums, a tourist snapped a picture of a woman in front of the tomb of voodoo queen Marie Laveau. A toddler swung on a wrought-iron gate nearby.

Forte jogged right and circled the cemetery, then turned back left on Orleans Avenue around Louis Armstrong Park. He wiped the sweat from his face on the sleeve of his torn gray tee-shirt. It was balmy today, one of those medium-humidity days that the city saw only in Spring and Fall, and then only sporadically. The park was scattered with frisbee chunkers, families on picnics, and lovers huddled on the benches. He let his mind drift as he settled into the rhythm of his running. He and Ruth had made the park a timeout place. The rule was that if they were on the park grounds, no arguing was allowed. He smiled at the memory. Many times they had barely made it into the park as a spat was escalating, then continued their stroll through the fight-free zone with Ruth shooting darts at him with her eyes while he pretended all was right with the world until she could maintain her ire no longer.

As he turned left on North Rampart and angled away from the park, Forte noticed a couple of men in shiny new orange windsuits jogging behind him. Where had they come from, he wondered. Both men looked to be in their 20's and in good shape. Forte took an unplanned left again, then turned right at the next block, glancing back to see if the men followed him. They had.

Forte maintained his tempo as he went right again then left on North Rampart down to Esplanade. He slowed as he headed toward the river, then resumed his speed as the orange suits turned the corner behind him. Party time. He picked up the pace as he doubled back through the Quarter toward his office. He could catch the bright color of their suits peripherally as he dodged through the people on the sidewalks.

He crossed the street between two taxis and glanced back. The taller of the two men had fallen back about half a block. When he got within two blocks of his office, he spied another man in a green windsuit leaning against the building across the street from his office. Their plan was obvious: they would catch him going into his office and force their way into The Refuge.

At the corner before his block, Forte casually took a right. He noticed the green suited man pushing himself away from the wall. Time to divide and conquer. He sprinted ahead and ducked into an alleyway and waited next to a garbage can. He could hear the splat-splat of his pursuer's steps. The man apparently had plenty of dash left.

Forte waited until the front pursuer, Orange Suit Number One, appeared at the entrance of the alley. Forte swung the metal lid of the garbage can. The man had a gun in his right hand. He spun to fire but too late. The lid caught his hand at the wrist.

The gun barked and Forte felt chips of brick stinging his neck. The pistol flew out of the alley back on to the sidewalk. Forte felt the kick on his thigh, a hard kick but partially deflected. Orange Suit One had recovered quickly but his right hand dangled at his side.

Forte shifted left and feinted a kick to the man's injured hand. The man lurched back. Forte's sweeping right kick caught his opponent behind the knees. He went down, his head smacking the cement. He was still.

Forte snatched the pistol from the concrete floor and came out of the alley in a low squat. At the left corner Orange Suit Number Two jogged around the corner wheezing, with a gun hanging from his hand. Forte was in a low shooting stance on one knee. He saw the man's arm whip up to level at him. Forte sighted at him but before he could fire he heard a boom from down the street. Orange Number Two suddenly jerked backwards and fell to the ground.

A bullet shattered the window of the abandoned storefront behind Forte. He swung toward the opposite corner of the street where the orange-suited man lay prone. The man in the green windsuit had a pistol with a silencer pointed at him. Forte heard a coughing noise and another bullet plinked on the bricks behind him. He leveled his gun at the man. Before he could shoot, Forte heard two more booms and saw Green Suit stumble back against the corner. He grabbed his shoulder and disappeared down the street.

Forte scrambled, head down, across the sidewalk away from the alley entrance. He ducked behind a parked car and peered up and down the side street.

At the far corner of the street stood a slender man with a rust-colored goatee. He casually slid a long-barreled revolver into a holster under his jacket. He pulled some sunglasses out of his jacket, put them on, looked at Forte and grinned. He turned and strolled down the sidewalk.

# Chapter 8

*Saturday, 4 p.m.*

The two little girls kneeled in the sandbox and made the dolls dance. Kyra's yellow playsuit looked bright against her coffee skin. She started singing, and the red-haired girl laughed, then joined in. The dolls danced faster and faster before the girls tumbled together in a jumble of giggles.

Forte stood on the walkway above the courtyard and watched them. He couldn't hear them from behind the one-way screen on the corridor and the girls couldn't see him. In the courtyard below, they could have been any two little girls on any playground.

Forte could see the reflection of Jackie Shaw, the shelter's manager, as she stood beside him looking down at the girls playing.

"No worries for them," he said. Even in the reflection, he could see the streak of premature white in her dark hair as she turned toward him.

"Our job to worry for them," she said.

Forte nodded and rubbed his neck. It felt wet.

"You're bleeding a little," she said.

"Yeah, couple pieces of brick got me," he said.

"You think it was the Colombians?" she asked.

46

"The police say the shooters aren't talking and they had no ID on them. But yeah, it was them," he said. "They're locked up now for a while."

She looked back at the girls playing. "And the other one, the one who shot at the Colombians ...?"

"One of Poochie's guys."

"You're sure?"

He looked down at her. "Yeah, I'm sure."

"Just so ... strange. I guess Poochie figured out his priorities," she said.

"Poochie's no dummy. But predictable he ain't," he said.

"Why does he think the Colombians are after Kyra?"

"He says they killed his brother – Kyra's dad, and that Kyra may have seen it happen. The Colombians had been supplying them, Poochie and his brother, before the two brothers made a new connection for their coke. His brother was found in his car, cut up pretty bad. I heard from some cop pals of mine that it looked like the Colombians' work."

She reached up and touched the back of his neck then showed Forte a red-stained finger. "Still bleeding. Come on, I've got a bandage in my office."

Forte followed her down the stairs and into her office. He sat in one of the guest chairs while she got a first aid kit from the closet. The scent of potpourri in the room blended with the odor of iodine as she opened the kit. A stack of empty cardboard boxes filled one corner of the room. Books lined the shelves along one wall. He scanned some of the spines of the books as he rested his elbows on her desk. A biography of Nadia Comaneci. A history of Olympic gymnastics. A Dean Koontz novel. A slim book titled For the Love of God: The Faith and Future of the American Nun.

He leaned forward as she applied some antibiotic ointment to his neck. "You unpacked fast," he said.

"Three weeks? An eternity if you've moved around as much as I have," she said.

"Yeah, I remember some from your resume. It was impressive." He felt the pressure of the bandage against his cuts as she taped it securely. "Sorry I haven't come by earlier to catch up with you."

Jackie snapped shut the first aid box. "No problem," she said. She put the box back in the closet and sat in the chair behind the desk. "So, catch up now." Her look was direct but not challenging. Friendly in a professional sort of way.

On the wall behind the desk hung a 1985 diploma from Boston College to Jacqueline Elise Shaw. Next to it, in a frame exactly the same size, was a photo of younger Jackie with short hair. She was wearing a gymnastics outfit with a medal strung around her neck on a blue ribbon. Standing next to her was a sturdy looking man who was smiling broadly.

She followed his gaze to the wall. "My proud Dad. I'd just won the regionals. Came this close to qualifying for the Olympics. He drove the guys crazy at the station house showing them that medal."

"He was a cop?"

"Yes. He just retired. My mom died when I was three. She was a big fan of the Kennedys like everyone else back home. So I was going to be named Jacqueline or Caroline. It was just him and me growing up. He taught me to shoot when I was six."

"Yeah, I remember that from the resume, the marksmanship awards."

She smiled. "Yeah. Great way to meet guys. Except I beat all of them."

"All of them?"

"Well, most of them, actually. It's how I met my future and past husband."

Forte looked from the wall photos to her. "Ahhh… future and past…"

Jackie smiled and straightened a piece of paper on the desk. "Yeah. He was a cop. I was a cop's daughter. You know how it goes. Dad warned me but…"

"You were smarter than Dad back then."

She nodded solemnly. "Of course. Somehow he got smarter later in life though. I married the guy. Stayed together 8 years. He ran off to Las Vegas. He got a great job in security at one of the casinos. Just didn't see the need to make room for me there."

"Did you want to go?"

She leaned back in her chair and rubbed her temples. "No. The relationship had started falling apart a couple of years before that."

He realized he had leaned forward; he settled back again in the chair. He paused. "Does it bug you to talk about it? Because we don't have to."

She looked at him calmly. "No, I don't mind really. I've dealt with that part of my life."

Sure, he thought. That's what we all say. He smoothed the bandage on his neck and kept quiet.

Jackie propped her right forearm on top of her head and with her left hand grasped her right wrist. "I found out I had ovarian cancer about three years after we were married. I was one of the lucky ones. The treatments knocked it out, but it turned out that I would never be able to have kids. The marriage went downhill from there."

"He was a sensitive male type, I gather."

She cocked her head. "You're being sarcastic, but in truth, yeah, he was sensitive at times. At other times, he was selfish and self-centered. Like all of us can be."

Forte raised his right hand. "No argument here on that one." He fingered the bandage on his neck. "And then… you became a nun."

Jackie laughed. "You want the whole story, don't you?"

"Just making conversation. Like I said, you don't have to tell anything really." He leaned back and studied the ceiling. "I mean, everyone's got something to hide, I guess."

She raised her eyebrows. "Good interrogation technique."

"Thanks. Now spill the beans."

Jackie nodded. "Okay, no biggie." She shifted and propped her sneakers on the desk. "I was a good Catholic girl like everyone in Boston. Had even thought about becoming a nun. After the divorce, I checked into it. It took a special dispensation and my ex had to sign papers but I did it. I was assigned to a delinquent girls program in New York City and then to an orphanage on the Mexican border in Reynosa. I loved it but eventually couldn't put up with the church politics."

"Bickering and power plays among the priests?" he asked.

"Worse," she said. "One of the priests was caught molesting little boys. The parish just covered it up." She shrugged. "I quit. That's that."

Forte nodded and said nothing.

Jackie took her feet down and rested her hands on the desktop in front of her. "So... now it's your turn."

"Oh?"

"Yep. Tell all."

"Guess I walked right into that one."

"That's right." Jackie sat and looked at him calmly, waiting for him to talk. Her hands were busy crumpling a sheet of paper.

He held up his hands in surrender. "Ok. You asked for it. What do you want to know?"

She stopped the paper-crumpling and leaned back in her chair. "All-righty. That's better. Let's see. You grew up in New Orleans?"

"Yup."

"Lived here all your life?"

"Nope."

"You're a fountain of information, you know that?"

He smiled. "Okay, okay. My parents were killed in a car accident when I was seven. We lived in Biloxi at the time. I came to live with my grandmother here in New Orleans. She managed a liquor store over on St. Charles. Great life for a kid, huh?"

Jackie kept silent.

"Actually, it was fun. She was great. Then she died when I was 13."

"Oh," Jackie said.

"Yeah, " he said. "Not good. A friend of my grandmother's took me in. Larue Hebert, a little Creole guy who owns a barber shop on Magazine. I lived with him until I joined the Navy right out of high school."

"No college, huh?"

Forte shifted in his chair. "No. Larue would have sent me to college probably if I would've asked. I got offered a couple of football scholarships at small schools but I opted for the Navy."

"And you became a Navy SEAL?"

"You been doing your homework."

"I can see the tattoo," she said, pointing to his left arm.

He looked down at the seal on his forearm. "Oh, right."

Jackie picked up the wadded paper. "See much combat?"

"Some. Panama, Desert Strike. Some super secret stuff. Shhhh."

She nodded. "So, how did you get from that, being a SEAL, to this?" She waved her arm over her head in a circle. "The Refuge. Protector and rescuer of children."

He smiled but there was something different around his eyes now. "That was my wife Ruth's idea. She dreamed about something we could do together, a mission we could share. She was a social worker."

Jackie set the paper wad on the desk and leaned back again.

Forte was focused on nothing in particular as he continued. "She was killed by a 14-year-old gang member. It was an accident, an initiation prank that went wrong. He shot her by accident. About five years ago."

Jackie was very still. "I'm sorry."

Forte remained expressionless. "Yeah, it was a bitch for sure." The room seemed colder now. "So, after trying to kill myself with booze and cocaine for a couple of years, I got sobered up and started this place. Ruth had inherited a lot of money and she specified in her will that most of it go to a foundation set up specifically to fund a shelter like this one."

Jackie nodded. "Yeah, I saw the plaque for the foundation in the lobby."

Someone put some Zydeco on the sound system. The spicy mixture of soul-flavored Cajun-French lyrics completely smothered the quietness of the office. Both Forte and Jackie smiled with relief.

"Just in time," she said. "It was getting too serious there for a minute."

The phone rang and for a brief moment it sounded like it was part of the song.

Jackie picked up the handset. "Hello?" She paused, then handed the receiver to Forte.

"Forte," he said. He listened for 10 seconds then handed the phone back to Jackie.

"Showtime," he said to her. "See you later."

He walked out of the office, down the hallway and passed through the ID scanners to get into the offices of Forte Security. At the front door, he paused, then opened it to a dozen camera flashes and a chorus of reporters.

# Chapter 9

*Saturday, 5 p.m.*

The image in the bathroom mirror was starkly different from the one that had appeared there earlier. Blue eyes, blond-white hair in a brush cut, bare face, no earring, sharp features. The man leaned forward and examined his image closely. Even the eyebrows had been dyed blond. It was close to his original coloring.

He resumed toweling dry his head as he walked into the den. On the television, the afternoon movie featured "Butch Cassidy and the Sundance Kid." Butch and The Kid are holed up above a saloon. They watch through a gash in the curtains as Sweet Face, the barkeep, tells the pursuing lawmen that the outlaw pair had ridden out of town. The lawmen ride away on their horses. "That Sweetface," Paul Newman as Butch says. "If he told *ME* that I just rode out of town, I'd believe him." The two outlaws tip their hats over their eyes and settle back for a snooze. Suddenly the clatter of hoofbeats rouses them. They jump up in time to see Sweetface pointing to their window, his face a mask of terror.

The television screen cut away to a news update from the local station. The screen showed a man standing on some steps in front of an office surrounded by reporters. A small sign on the wall behind the man bore the words "Forte Security." The wide camera angle showed the worn brick of the renovated office and some gawkers standing under the street sign on the corner. The word "LIVE" was superimposed on the top right corner of the picture. A voice-over from an off-camera newscaster blanketed the on-camera shouts of the reporters. "Just an hour ago, security specialist Al Forte was attacked by three men just two blocks from his office. Two of the men were subdued and the third assailant escaped. Police spokespersons have been unable to identify the suspects in custody, but they deny that this attack has anything to do with Forte's involvement in the murder investigation of Dr. Tyson Lamberth, the abortion doctor who was killed early this morning at his clinic. Forte was hired to provide security for the Lamberth family after Dr. Lamberth's murder."

Outside the house in Gretna, a lawnmower droned somewhere down the street. Inside, the man had stopped toweling his hair as he watched the news.

The news camera cut to a closeup of Al Forte. The killer studied the face. It had seemed like a fairly ordinary face from a distance. Now you could see the set of the jaw and the strange yellow eyes. Above the right eye was an X-shaped scar.

"In our business, we make some enemies," Forte told the microphones. "It's not easy to sort them out sometimes." The reporters immediately assaulted him with shouted questions, sounding like a pack of dogs yelping as they circled the tree where a raccoon smiled down at them. One voice rose sharply with a question. "Mr. Forte, do you think the murder of Dr. Lamberth was justified, considering your views on abortion?"

The killer realized he had squatted in front of the television set, the towel draped over his shoulder as he peered at the screen.

Forte's brow furrowed at the question as he looked at the reporter who asked it. "First, let me say that I am not involved in the investigation of Dr. Tyson's murder. The FBI is handling that. My company has been hired to provide security protection for the Lamberth family. And second, even though it is true that I oppose abortion, I don't think that the doctor's murder was justified. We have a justice system here in America and, like it or not, we have to live with its processes or change them within our democratic system." The media crowd erupted in questions again but Forte had escaped into the office again.

The killer spat at the television screen. "Fool," he said aloud. "In your heart, you don't really believe that."

He stood and walked into the bedroom and put the towel in a hamper. In the closet, he slid aside the shirts and pants on hangers. In the wall was a safe. He spun the dial of the combination lock. Seven right, 14 left, 52 right. The door of the safe clicked open. He reached in and brought out two zippered carrying cases and a leather cleaning kit. He walked back through the den. The television had switched back to the movie. He turned it off and turned on the stereo system. He examined the CDs and pulled one from the rack. "The Unfinished Symphony" by Schubert. He fed the disc to the machine and waited for the first strains of the orchestra to drown out the distant hum of the lawnmower.

He walked over to the dining room table in its alcove next to the den. From the corner of the table he took several newspapers from a stack. He spread them over the table at least four pages thick. He set the zippered cases on the newspapers next to the cleaning kit. Out of the zippered cases he took an Army issue Colt 45 automatic and a Ruger .22 caliber with an eight-inch barrel that had been machine-grooved on the barrel-end so you could screw on a silencer.

He thought about Forte as he opened the cleaning kit, assembled the cleaning rod and threaded a clean white cotton patch through the notched tip of the rod. Forte was a traitor to his own beliefs. Worse, he was spouting off on TV about his double-faced notion of justice.

Where was the justice for the millions of unborn children who had been murdered in their mothers' wombs? The government's idea of justice had led them to slaughter. Yet, you, Mr. Forte, stand there and say that lethal force is not justified when protecting a child? Who else will protect them?

He took a bottle of nitro solvent from the case, then dipped the cotton patch into the bottle. He picked up the .22 pistol and stabbed the cleaning rod through the bore of the pistol. In and out. In and out. He realized he was cleaning in tempo to the Schubert piece. He closed his eyes. In and out, in and out.

The smell of the solvent soothed him. It always made him feel that order was being restored. Order for the guns he cleaned. Order for his world.

# Chapter 10

*Saturday, 9 p.m.*

"Thanks for stirring up things with that question about 'justified murder' in front of the cameras," Forte said to the slight man on the other side of the booth. Jonathan Brach smiled as he sliced a bite of redfish on the dinner plate and popped it into his mouth.

"You are quite welcome," Brach said. "I figured you would rather hear the question from a friend than from one of those TV bozos."

A third man stood next to the booth where Forte and Brach sat, holding a leather menu with "Mack's" on the cover. His bulk blocked the light from the bell-shaped ceiling light.

"Revenge of the dweebs," he said, jabbing a thick thumb in Brach's direction. "That's why he became a reporter. So he could pay us jocks back for our glory-hogging days of high school yore."

The small man put a hand over his mouth in mock-yawn. "Mack, you might better sit down and rest now. That earth-shaking insight you just shared surely must have drained all the blood from your miniscule brain." He paused and put his fingers over his mouth. "Oops. I used a word with more than two syllables."

Mack Quadrie solemnly held up a right hand the size of a dinner plate and scratched the corner of his eye with his middle finger. "Yes," he said, "I was right proud of that remark." The three men laughed. The giant walked over to shake hands with another patron of his restaurant. He moved with the grace of the ex-pro tackle he was.

Forte watched Mack walk away from the table as he lit a Checkers. "He's done well for himself, hasn't he?"

Brach lowered his coffee cup. "Yes, he has. I'm proud of him. Of course, if you tell him I said that, you will never again reap the magnificent informational harvest that is yours courtesy of the Times-Picayune. Via yours truly, of course."

"Such power."

"Yes, bow before me."

Forte let his gaze casually sweep over the crowd at the restaurant. In his days as a Navy SEAL on reconnaissance, he had been trained to look not for a particular sign of danger but for the thing that didn't seem to fit into the normal background of the situation. Nothing seemed out of place here tonight. A large party of people in business suits and Chanel dresses had pushed four tables together to half-fill the center of the room. In the booths along the opposite wall, couples and foursomes sipped wine and waited for their jambalaya or gumbo or one of Mack's dinner specials. Two tables away, a tall man with a white-blond military-style haircut smiled across their table at a woman in an evening gown, who was listening closely to some joke the man was spinning for her. The woman tilted her head with a perfectly cultured laugh.

Brach snapped his fingers. "Your fingers are about to be burned."

Forte re-focused on his friend, then ground out his cigarette in the ashtray on the table.

"Tough habit to break," Brach said. "I remember."

"Yeah, big fun. That was cig number three for today. And I miss it already."

"Progress though."

"So they say." Forte picked up his fork and pushed the remaining al dente broccoli around on his plate then set the fork down and picked up his coffee.

"That incident this afternoon spook you?"

"Just being watchful."

Brach sipped his coffee silently as he watched the people stroll past the front windows of the restaurant on Bourbon Street. The old street lamps outside were just beginning to flicker to life in the dwindling twilight.

The reporter carefully set his coffee cup on the table. "You know, Al, you are different now. I mean, compared to how you used to be. Sometimes I wonder if you know that people notice that," Brach said.

"Different, huh," Forte said.

"Yeah, I mean different from the way you were in high school. I mean, we were friends then but ... you know, you had this kind of toughness, this barrier that only let people so close. And when you got out of the Navy, it was even thicker, more impenetrable -- the barrier, I mean."

Forte nodded. "I can see that."

Brach leaned forward. "It's just that... since Ruth's passing and everything... you seem more..." He paused and looked up at nothing as he searched his mind for a word. "You are more vulnerable. Not in a bad way. I mean, you are obviously still tough and all that or you couldn't do the work you do. And we still joke around like we always did, you, me and Mack. You are just... more approachable, I suppose." He leaned back. "It's something I've meant to say for a while, since you..." His voice trailed off. "You wouldn't think a wordsmith like me would have such a hard time expressing himself. Anyway, it's a good thing."

Forte smiled. "Thanks. It's a one-day-at-a-time thing." He saw that the intensity on his friend's face remained. "I don't mean to simplify it, Jon, really. When I was in treatment, I got thrown a lot of the stuff that I thought was just a load of psycho-babble crap. But some of it was on target, for me. I had to admit that I wasn't on this planet alone, able to control any situation I encountered. Hell, I couldn't even control myself. The cocaine taught me that." He paused and thought for a moment. "But, somehow, coming to that conclusion, that I wasn't in charge of the world, started to give me some peace. And I try to get a little more of it every day." He laughed softly. "Some speech, huh?"

Brach's face had softened. "Yeah, a good one."

Forte clapped his hands together and a few people at nearby tables looked up from their plates. "Enough of this tender spit-swappin'. Tell me if there's any more news on the Lamberth murder investigation."

The reporter grinned. "Yeah, we wouldn't want you to come across as an actual human being." He motioned to a waiter for more coffee. "The Fibbee's are tearing their hair out on this one. Big pressure all the way up to the new Attorney General. Because he's a conservative, and because of all that flak he caught at his confirmation hearings, he's bearing down on this case. Rosie Dent is catching a lot of flak in her new job as AIC, Agent in Charge."

Forte waved a hand impatiently and waited for the waiter to pour more coffee and leave the table. "Yeah, yeah, politics excites me so much. Tell me if they know anything else about the killer."

The reporter grinned again and slowly stirred sugar into his cup. "Okay, okay. I take back that other sappy stuff I said. Here's the scoop. A city cop across the river found the doctor's assistant on a bench in Algiers about 1:30 this afternoon. The guy, David Butler, was under some newspapers with his mouth, wrists and ankles bound with duct tape. He said he'd been mugged when he went out jogging early this morning, just as he was coming out of his apartment. He never saw what hit him. His car, a beat-up blue Pinto, is gone.

"The other clinic employee is the one they haven't caught up with yet, Brent Garrison." He picked up his cup then set it down. "He's the main suspect now. His fingerprints were all over the clinic but that's not surprising; he worked there. The FBI finished running his prints through their computers and can't find a match, so he has no criminal record. Some agents have been scouring the San Fernando Valley in California where Garrison was from."

He paused to sip more coffee as Forte motioned for him to continue. "You're going to love this: Brent Garrison, the real one, died eight months ago. He was a security cop for some California state government office. He had retired last year at age 36 because of heart problems. And the kicker is this: some hacker had gone into the government computers and tinkered with his records. His death certificate had been erased from the system. The FBI had to bring in some file clerk manager on his day off at a family reunion to even track down the paper copy of the death certificate." He grinned. "So who was the guy working at the clinic using Garrison's name? They don't know yet."

Forte leaned back in the corner of the booth and absorbed the information. "So, the killer stole the identity of a dead man, got himself hired at the clinic and worked there for six months before killing the doctor." He unconsciously traced the scar above his eye. "He was committed."

The blond man at the next table was smiling as he perused the menu.

"He must've been a Nazi. Like those guys who hold their hand over a flame to prove their commitment."

Snap. The blond man closed his menu abruptly.

Forte realized he had been looking at the man as he listened to Brach talk. The man was still smiling but there was something different, around the edges of the smile. Forte looked at the woman across from the blond man. Her face seemed frozen into a look of forced pleasantness. Was he imagining it? Tiny lines of tension grew from the corner of her mouth.

On the street outside the front window of Mack's, a marching band erupted into "As the Saints Go Marchin' In." Even though it was a couple months past Mardi Gras, local school bands were occasionally hired by companies to lead their convention groups in mini-parades. As the high school band swept past the windows, half the people in Mack's crowded up to the window to watch. A few people rushed out on the sidewalk to catch beads and doubloons emblazoned with the name of the company that had created the makeshift parade. People in business suits and party hats followed the band past the windows and down the street to another restaurant.

Brach turned and looked out the windows, then returned to his coffee. "Tourists," he muttered.

Forte said nothing. The crowd withdrew from the window and filed past his booth on their way back to their tables. His view was blocked for a moment.

"Hey," said Brach. "That answer you gave for the cameras earlier. Do you really believe that? Or was it just a media-bite?"

Forte looked at his friend. "What?"

"The stuff you said. About our justice system being responsible for the punishment of the murderer."

"I said that society has to live with the laws we have or change them. I meant that."

"But, really, deep down, don't you think the doctor deserved what he got? I mean, if you believe that the fetus is a human being, then you believe he was killing children. And if you were in that room, would you have stopped the doctor from killing that child?"

As Forte thought about the question, he tried to see the table with the blond man. Two woman were standing between his booth and the table talking about their dessert possibilities. He looked back at Brach.

"Off the record?" Forte asked.

Brach feigned a look of pain. "Mi compadre, you stab my heart."

Forte said nothing.

Brach smiled. "Okay, off the record, of course."

Forte nodded. "In that exact situation, if I had happened to be in the room somehow, I would have stopped him. I don't know if I would have tried to kill him."

"You don't know?"

Forte looked at his friend's face for a long moment. "No. I don't know."

"What about the woman? What about her so-called reproductive rights?"

"What about them?"

Brach sighed. "You know what I mean. Doesn't the woman have the right to decide what happens to her own body?"

"You know, ever since I was called about the Lamberth thing, people have been questioning me about this one way or another."

"I'm just interested. I know you have strong views on this."

"I do." He paused. The women were finally moving out of the way. "I just don't want to completely dismiss the woman's rights. I used to be so blunt in my opinion on this that women would scream at me for being a chauvinistic pig. And even now I don't claim to be able to understand what a woman would go through in her mind. I mean, as she was deciding to have an abortion.

"But after all the politics and emotions are talked to death, I still believe it is wrong."

Brach said nothing.

Forte searched his friend's eyes.

He looked back across the restaurant.

The blond man and his dinnermate were gone.

# Chapter 11

A squirrel tiptoed along the top of the eight-foot brick wall that surrounded the Lamberths' house. It slowed and stopped as it examined a tree limb that stretched from the massive oak in the center of the lawn. The closest branch had been stylishly manicured to end more than a man's height away from the wall. The squirrel furtively looked all around him, then bunched his hind legs under himself and sprang toward the leaves at the end of the branch. His front paws snagged and caught the tip of the branch. He bobbed and swayed like a drunken trapeze artist then pulled himself onto the branch and scampered up the limb and around the girth of the tree trunk.

Forte watched the squirrel from the back patio outside the garden room where he had first met with Freida Lambert and Mr. Tolan. He slowly sucked on cigarette number four. The tobacco smoke could not quite hide the aroma from the wisteria next to the patio. The smell was a contrast from the usual stale whiskey-sweat-garbage smell of the Quarter. As he stood and smoked, Forte had not made up his mind which he liked better. From the windows above and behind him, the improvisations of Phish in concert poured out of Hallee's stereo and into the night air. At least the kid had some good sense of music, Forte thought.

He had tapped on Hallee's door when he came on duty a half-hour earlier as he was conducting his first complete walk-through of the house. The second-floor room had only recently been converted from three rooms, the walls knocked down to create a hangar of a bedroom. Three windows overlooked the garden in the backyard, the center one with a window seat.

A girl with short auburn hair was curled on the window seat clutching a stuffed tiger as she looked out at the spotlighted backyard. A breeze made the curtains dance across the screenless window.

"Will they stay on all night?" she asked without turning around.

Forte looked around the room. "Will what stay on?"

Hallee lifted a hand and pointed a purple fingernail at the window. "Those spotlights in the backyard. I won't be able to sleep."

"No, we are testing them now. They are automatic detection lights."

"So, they come on if someone tries to break in."

"Yes."

She turned and looked at him, her arms still locked around the stuffed animal. "The people who killed my dad? If they try to break in?"

Forte stood in the center of the room. He had been studying the layout, memorizing where everything was: the canopy bed, the entertainment center crammed with a TV-VCR combo, a stereo system with four speakers, a Sony Playstation and stacks of videos and CD's and books and electronic games. Next to the bed on the floor lay a pair of Nike sneakers and a pair of ballet slippers. A large globe on a stand sat at the end of the desktop.

He looked at Hallee. Her face showed no emotion but her brown eyes shimmered.

"For anyone," he said. "Anyone without a special invitation from me."

She said nothing as she rubbed her cheek against the tiger's fake fur.

"You don't look like the others," she said.

"Oh really," he said.

"Yeah, they are pretty grim. The cops."

"Grim, huh?"

"Yeah," she said. "But you seem … I dunno. Cool."

"That's me. Mr. Cool."

One corner of the girl's mouth twitched. "Don't make fun of me." She shifted on the cushion. "Nice tattoo."

Forte lifted his forearm. "Thanks."

"My mom has one. Not where you can see it though." The other corner of her mouth twitched.

"I'm sure she appreciates you sharing that information."

She shrugged. "It's nothing weird. Just a butterfly."

Forte scanned the room a moment longer then turned from the door to the hallway. "If you need anything, just call," he said.

Hallee just looked at him, then nodded.

Forte had continued his rounds. Freida Lamberth had been talking to an Episcopal priest in the garden room so he had stepped outside. He walked along the wall that completely surrounded the house. The driveway gate on the side of the house was locked shut and another solid-wall security gate was positioned behind it. Even a small animal couldn't walk onto the grounds. All he had to do was watch for the attack of the flying squirrels coming over the walls.

From the corner of his eye he caught a movement in the garden room. The priest had come to his feet. He hugged the widow and glanced out at the lone figure standing on the patio. Freida led the man out of the room.

After a moment Forte heard the security gate slide open, then snap shut behind the priest. A moment later he heard the click of heels on the stone walkway leading around to the patio where he stood exhaling the dwindling pleasure of number four.

"Got one for me?" Freida said as she approached. Her voice sounded even more hoarse than it had earlier in the day. Sometime during the day she had changed into a simple black dress with no jewelry. Her hair was pulled back into a bun. As he watched her step close for the cigarette, Forte could see the tiny holes in her earlobes where the earrings had been. In the strong light of the security lamps, her face still looked naked of any makeup.

"A warning to you," he said, lighting the Checkers in her mouth. "These are not premium brand."

She inhaled and the tip of the cigarette glowed red. She grimaced. "That's the understatement of the day." She took another deep drag and waved him to one of the patio chairs. She sat down and crossed her legs, tilted her head back and released a plume of smoke above her head. The closest security light showed up as streaks of silver in the smoke.

Forte checked his watch. "The timer on the test for the lights should be going off... just about..."

The lights shut off, plunging the patio into darkness.

"Now."

Forte could barely make out Freida's outline behind the glow of the cigarette.

"How are you holding up?" he asked.

Freida kept her head pressed against the tall back of the chair. He couldn't tell if her eyes were open or closed. "I don't know," she said. She put her free hand behind her head and rubbed her neck.

Forte's cigarette had burned down nearly to the filter. He held it up with his left hand and flicked the embers away with his right index finger. He put the cooled filter tip in his pocket. Some different music now drifted out of Hallee's window above, something he didn't recognize. Slower, softer, violins and flutes stirred together in a synthesized new age soup. Maybe Enya.

"I saw the news earlier. About you being attacked," she said. "Will that affect your work for me?"

"No," he said.

"Good." She had stopped rubbing her neck. "What was it about really?"

"We aren't sure. Probably had something to do with the shelter. The Refuge."

"Yes, I had imagined it did."

His eyes were adjusting to the darkness, and he could make out her features now. "You know, Hallee would be much safer there," he said.

"At The Refuge?"

"Yes."

She shook her head and a strand of hair escaped from the bun. "No. It is better that we are here. Together."

He nodded. "As you wish, ma'am. It will be fine."

Freida tilted her head toward him. "Ma'am? Please! I'm no older than you are."

"Sorry. It was my Grandmama's good manners speaking."

"She raised you, didn't she, after your parents died?"

It was Forte's turn to tilt his head. "You know about that, eh?"

"I know a lot about you," she said. She inhaled another drag and held it, then pursed her lips and blew out the cloud of white. "My husband had Mr. Tolan do a background check on you months ago. He was considering hiring your company for security for Hallee even … before all this. Tolan talked him out of it."

"But you disagreed with Tolan."

"Yes. He means well but he lets his politics get in the way of good judgement."

"Sometimes almost any little thing can get in the way of good judgement."

Freida sunk lower in the patio chair and looked up at the clouded sky. "Truer words..." Her voice floated up and away, smaller than it had been. She sniffed once and cleared her throat.

"My husband was not perfect," she said. "He was unfaithful to me and he was often preoccupied with his work. But, with all that, he loved me, in his way. I know he did. And I loved him. And now he is gone." Her voice cracked. In the semi-dark, Forte could see her shoulders shaking but he could not hear the crying.

He waited quietly. It was one of the things he learned from wise Larue. "When there ain't no words that can help, almost any word can hurt," the little man had counseled him in what amounted to a long speech one day after Al had smart-mouthed his way into a two-day suspension from junior high school.

Her shaking stopped after a few moments. "I'm sorry. All day ... so many people here ..."

Forte leaned up and patted her hand. "It's hard answering the questions."

The night was quiet. Hallee's windows were dark now.

Freida stood up and let her cigarette drop to the imported tiles of the patio. She stepped on it with the toe of her high heel pump and ground it out. "Sometimes," she said, "there don't seem to be any answers." She walked into the house.

Forte watched her go then looked up at the sky. Oh, there are answers to the pain, he thought. Just not always the right ones. But when the chance comes along to make the hurt go away for even a few minutes, you forget about right or wrong. You just think about the here and now and the chance to escape. He remembered that feeling every morning when his eyes opened and every night when they closed and all the moments in between. The memory of that sweet escape, despite its insanity, was not always strong. Sometimes it lived way back on the edge of his consciousness. But it seemed like it was always there, looking at him from across the distance like a wolf beyond rifle range, a wolf with its teeth exposed in a cruel smile. Waiting.

Right now, he wanted Checkers number five. But he would force himself to delay that pleasure for a while.

He got up and went inside. He locked the doors and reset the security system. Anything more than a few feet tall that moved anywhere in the yard would instantly trigger the outside spotlights and the shrieking of alarms.

# Chapter 12

*Saturday, 10:30 p.m.*

On the monitor in the van, Forte looked small and tired. But that was just an illusion, the killer knew. A man with Forte's reputation would have the combination of training and instincts that could make for danger.

The killer, dressed completely in black, sipped juice from a bottle. But then again, he thought, anyone can be fooled.

He had watched Forte and Freida Lamberth chatting on the patio. It had been hard to see them when the security lights shut off. But he had seen the cigarettes glowing and knew they were still there. The microphones he had planted months before were working perfectly. He could hear everything. The woman's remark about her husband's unfaithfulness made him smile to himself. Why wouldn't the doctor fool around? He was accountable to no one and believed he could "fix" any inconvenience caused by his dalliances.

The grief in Freida's voice actually made him feel uneasy a bit, but he considered it a casualty of war, that kind of grief. Besides, it was all part of the plan and the plan must be carried out.

The van was parked behind a bar on St. Charles, six blocks from the Lamberth home. Anyone driving by would see a beat-up beige van with "Nance Plumbing" emblazoned on the side in royal blue block letters a foot tall. Inside the van, everything was state-of-the-art. The killer sat on a rolling stool facing a console of electronic equipment. The images on three tiny monitors flashed views of all four sides of the Lamberth home, all three entrances into the house, the kitchen, the den, the stairway, the hallway leading past Hallee Lamberth's bedroom on the second floor, and the third floor landing outside Freida Lamberth's bedroom. The miniscule remote video cameras he had planted at the Lamberth house were working perfectly, beaming the images to his receiver in the truck and giving him knowledge of every movement in and around the house. The cameras had been in place for more than three months, lying dormant except for a few tests until being automatically triggered for tonight's mission.

A police scanner tuned to the New Orleans band was bolted to the wall of the van next to his head. It squawked and he listened for any indication that the dispatcher was talking to a police unit nearby. Satisfied that he wasn't, he pushed away from the console and glided backward on the small rolling chair across the rubber floor mat until his back rested against the opposite wall of the van. He rested there, watching the monitors. He looked down and flexed his hands. The light of the monitors cast a greenish hue on his skin.

This was the part of the mission that had bothered him when it had first been planned. It was one thing to kill a murderer in the act of defending an unborn child. But the Lamberth girl, she was innocent. He rubbed his eyes. He reminded himself that the big picture would be served by this act. It was just the actual execution of it that bothered him. But it had to be done.

He would make it quick so the girl would not be afraid.

He reached down and picked up the old black canvas duffel bag with the letters "CPD-SWAT" on it. He moved the bag closer to the counter next to the electronic equipment and opened it. Reaching

73

into the bag, he started unpacking it, neatly stacking its contents on the countertop: the .45 automatic, the .22 automatic, the screw-on silencer for the .22, two shoulder holsters for the guns, a black Kevlar bulletproof vest, a coil of black half-inch nylon rope, a small remote device with two rows of buttons about the size of a TV remote, a small empty black backpack, a pair of thin black gloves and a black cotton ski-mask with holes for the eyes and the mouth.

He clicked on a small light above the counter top. The van's side and back windows were painted black and a curtain was drawn across the compartment behind the driver's seat to prevent any light inside the van from escaping. It was the inattention to details that got you caught.

He pushed aside the other items from the canvas bag and closely examined the remote control. Tacked to a small bulletin board above the counter top was a diagram on a sheet of paper. It showed the exact function of each of the remote's buttons. He took out a piece of paper from a drawer under the counter. He quickly drew up the layout of the buttons on the remote and, without looking at the diagram on the wall, jotted down the function for each button. When he finished, he checked his answers against the diagram on the board. Perfect. He knew it would be; he'd tested himself dozens of times already.

The police scanner squawked again and he listened, then relaxed. Everything was in place. When it was time he would move the van closer to the Lamberth house.

He reached up above the monitors and pressed the "Play" button on a small CD player he had strapped to a metal shelf there. He rolled his chair against the wall and leaned back again. The music started. Dvorak's "New World Symphony."

He watched the monitors flick from one image to another.

And waited until the time to act.

# Chapter 13

With the lights in the house turned off, Forte – dressed completely in black – was virtually invisible from where he sat in the corner of the den. He had moved one of the heavy wooden dining room chairs to that particular corner because it was the one spot where he could see three sides of the house. To his left was a wide hallway that led to a sunroom off the kitchen with a bank of windows overlooking the back yard. To his right were the ceiling-high windows that looked out into the front yard. In front of him was a picture window that faced the side yard leading all the way along the driveway to the security gate. Anyone coming into the house would have less than three seconds to adjust his eyes from the blinding glare of the outside security lights to the darkness of the house.

About two-and-a-half seconds too long, Forte mused. His main weapon rested lightly across his knees: a Remington 870 shotgun with a black matte finish, a black molded plastic pump grip, a pistol grip, and an 18-and-a-half inch barrel. The first of the seven 12-gauge shells in the magazine was filled with hard rubber balls intended at best to stun an assailant and, at worst, to break ribs or other bones. The other six  shotgun shells were loaded with lead pellets. These were designed for close-up combat: only someone in the immediate vicinity would die from the shotgun blast. None of the pellets would travel through walls far enough to escape the house and accidentally kill a neighbor a quarter mile away as a rifle bullet would do.

All lights in the house had been doused and the music silenced more than two hours earlier. Like all of the renovated mansions in the Garden District, the Lamberth house emitted its share of creaks and groans. Forte watched the limbs of the giant oak tree in the back sway slightly in the wind that had kicked up since the afternoon. The clouds had paraded in front of a one-quarter moon for the past hour. Now they formed a bank of blackness, making the leaves of the oak a solid swatch of gray-green instead of the individual reflectors of green-silver light from the moon that they had been just an hour earlier. The edges of the single leaves were barely discernable now even to his night-ready eyes.

Forte had developed his own regimen for these types of all-night watches. He would conduct walk-throughs in the house at irregular intervals each hour: at 13, 27, and 44 after the hour in the first hour of the watch, then 14, 28, and 45 the next, then back to the first intervals and so forth through the night. With the expensive security system that the Lamberths had in place, he knew his watchfulness was almost certainly overkill. But it was his way of doing things. And besides, his regimen would keep him occupied and alert during the long hours of darkness.

During his times at rest in the chair, he let his mind roam over the house and the yard, imagining that it was free from his body and could see everywhere. The biggest challenge of this type of assignment was the monotony. Even if you did not succumb to sleepiness, you could easily let your mind wander along some mental trail that put you in the kind of conscious-dream zone that would rob you of alertness. A split second's loss in response time could kill him. Which would bring death to everyone in the house.

Forte shifted in his chair and adjusted the Velcro strap that held his bullet-proof vest close to his ribs. He checked his watch, then stood and stretched, holding the shotgun over his head as though he were about to wade through a slimy pond in Central America. He pulled a small flashlight out of a zippered pocket on the leg of his pants and clicked it on, then walked around the perimeter of the den, pausing to look out the windows at the yard. The wind made the shrubs shimmy in the corner of the front yard. The taller trees were less affected by the gusts but now even they bobbed their thick limbs like a portly woman doing water calisthenics. Forte watched the trees carefully. Nothing seemed out of place.

He continued his tour of the downstairs, moving through the hallway to the garden room overlooking the flowers. Except for the darkness, the garden room looked the same as it had earlier in the day, the architecture and fashion magazines fanned out perfectly on the coffee table. He went into the downstairs study where Tyson Lamberth's computer still hummed. The desk around the computer was neat but not arranged with a decorative eye. A brochure on some Caribbean island stuck out of a stack of papers at an angle. He went into each of the downstairs bathrooms, checking in the closets and shower stalls. He doubled back to the stairway and moved up to the second floor, listening to his dampened steps on the carpeted runners. The renovation crew must have done a fantastic job tightening the stairs, he thought. He could hear very few creaks as he walked, and the ones he heard sounded no louder than the regular creaks caused by the wind rushing against the old mansion.

Forte walked along the second story landing, a polished mahogany rail to his left overlooking the den below. He approached the door of the guest bedroom and opened it, his shotgun held at an angle to the floor. He beamed his light under the bed, in the closet, in the attached bathroom. Nothing.

He walked back out of the room and listened. The wind seemed to be blowing harder now, hinting at a storm. He walked to Hallee's door and pushed it open.

A flash of movement across the room. Forte silently whirled and dropped to one knee, the shotgun level now. His flashlight was at arm's length from his body, to lure gunfire away from the center of his body.

The curtain over the center window billowed out and receded. The girl had left the window open.

In the bed, the girl slept, her breathing deep and steady.

Forte let the beam of the flashlight travel along the wall as he remained on one knee. Satisfied that it was just the wind, he rose and walked over the window. He could see the first drops of rain from the incoming storm hitting the shingles of the garage as the roof slanted down from Hallee's room. He latched the window and pulled the curtain closed again.

The girl shifted in the bed but did not wake up. Forte went out of the room, leaving the door slightly ajar.

He stood on the second floor landing for a moment and listened to the sounds of rushing wind and drumming rain as the storm continued to build outside.

He went up the stairs to the third floor landing. The master bedroom with an attached reading room, walk-in closets and a Jacuzzi bathroom occupied the entire third floor of the house. Forte walked past the bedroom door and listened without going inside. No sounds came from the bedroom. He walked back down the stairs, through the dining room and into the kitchen.

He moved the shotgun so it would hang from its strap around his neck and lie along his back. He opened the refrigerator, took out a pitcher of orange juice and set it on the countertop where he and the city cop had stood talking about 14 hours earlier. To Forte, it seemed like much more time had passed since then. He took a tumbler out of one of the grass-front cabinets above the countertop and poured it full of orange juice.

The fluttering curtain in Hallee's room had spooked him just enough to release some adrenaline into his system. He still felt it. The event did not annoy him. On the contrary, after he saw that the girl was safe, he had felt a tiny bit of satisfaction at his response. It was exactly right, just as he had first been trained years ago. And just as his yearly training retreats had been designed to produce. He did not want his alertness to wane when the adrenaline went way. The orange juice would help.

He sipped the juice and watched the rain drum against the kitchen window. Without any light to shine through its transparence, the rivulets of raindrops ran like mercury on the panes of glass. Lightning flashed and the water sparkled in the blue streak of light. The darkness dropped again even more heavily now. Forte counted. One-thousand-one, one-thousand-two, one-thousand-three... The thunder crashed. The storm was close.

Twenty-four hours, Forte thought. Sometimes they filled a day that seemed the same as the day before that and the day before that and the days of weeks and months and years before that. Then again, sometimes there came a stretch of 24 hours that completely changed your life. For good or bad. The trouble was you never had any clue whether the upcoming day would be the same-old-same-old kind or the kind that tore your life apart as quickly and effortlessly as a lightning bolt splits a Sequoia.

Twenty-four hours earlier he had been standing in the gallery after the meeting, listening to his sponsor Manning Laird tell a tale of alcoholic mishap from his days as a merchant marine. "When I woke up, a pair of Hong Kong hookers were standing in the alley fighting over my pants. They thought I was dead. I sat up and yelled, 'Hey, is this Oahu?' It scared them so bad they dropped the pants and took off. I didn't catch up with my boat until it had docked back in San

Francisco." The small cluster of people around him burst into that special kind of laughter reserved for those who had, at one time or another, drunk from that common cup of hopelessness.

In the 24 hours since, a man had died, a baby saved. A husband gone, a father's life extinguished. He stood in the dead man's kitchen, filling a role for the simple reason that he could do it. And somewhere, people still slept peacefully or made love or danced the night away.

The kitchen lit up again as the lightning flashed. One-thousand-one, one-thou…Boom came the thunder. The storm was almost on top of them.

Forte tilted the tumbler back and drained it, then stepped to the sink and rinsed it.

A scream came from upstairs.

Before the scream had spent itself Forte was at the foot of the stairs. He clicked the safety to the off position as he swung the shotgun around to face forward and bolted up the stairs three at a time.

He went through Hallee's door low and rolled to the left. He came up and swung the barrel across the room. Nothing moved.

Hallee rolled over in her bed and mumbled something. She immediately went back to sleep.

Forte slowly came up from his crouch. He shined the flashlight across the room, in the closet and the bathroom again. Nothing.

Crash. The sound came from upstairs.

He ran up to the third floor and paused just as another scream came from the master bedroom.

He kicked open the door and went in low again.

A lamp from the nightstand had been swept onto the floor, where it rolled lazily on the carpet. Forte trained the shotgun on the movement of the lamp. He swept the room with the light.

Freida Lamberth lay thrashing across the bed diagonally, the sheet and covers half off of her. A low moan of terror came from her throat. Then another scream, the hoarse kind of scream that sounded like it would hurt your throat for days afterward.

Forte quickly darted past the bed. He crouched and flung open the doors of the reading room, the bathroom, the closets. Nothing. He looked out the window. The rain was pounding the house now but the security lights in the yard below were still off.

He walked back to the bed. The woman's silk nightgown had ridden high on her thigh. Forte bent over to pull the sheet back over her. Lightning flashed just as the woman twisted in the bed again. He could see a tiny butterfly high on her hip. The tattoo's bright red, yellow and blue was surreal, like a dream itself. Then the room was dark once more.

He clicked the safety on and bent and put the shotgun on the floor. He pulled the sheets over her bare legs. The thunder crashed. She screamed again and bolted upright in the bed.

"You killed him!" she screamed, flailing with her fists.

One punch caught him on the cheek before he could catch her wrists and hold her still. "Shhhh," he said. "It's a nightmare. You were dreaming."

Freida struggled and made a guttural sound like an animal in pain. Then Forte felt the fight go out of her. She was strong but now she seemed to shrink in his arms. She held onto him sobbing. He could feel hot tears trickling down his neck to his shirt collar as she pressed against him.

He made a small attempt to release her but she clung to him. Her crying was mixed with a racking moan he had heard before. From his own mouth.

He held her. A few moments passed and the sobbing died away. He could feel her breath steady against his neck. She made no noise now.

He became aware of the heat of her body against him. The thin silk of her nightgown slid beneath his hands as she moved. He could feel her lips against his neck. Her breathing was faster now.

Her teeth grazed his chin. His arms still surrounded her. "Freida," he said, his voice hoarse. He pulled his head back slightly to see her face.

She kissed him, frantic and deep, the breath from her nostrils hot on his face. He tensed. He kissed her back.

He could hear a low moan as they pressed together. The straps of her gown were off her shoulders. The press of their embrace pushed it lower.

He kissed her neck. His skin was burning now. *So long. It had been so long.*

Suddenly he froze.

"No," he said. "Not…"

She lunged toward him, grabbing his head in her hands, trying to kiss him. "Please," she said, her voice trembling.

He gently took her wrists in his hands and held them.

The lightning flashed again. One-thousand-one, one-thousand-two, one-thousand-three, one-thou… The thunder followed. The storm was moving past now.

She struggled against him now. In the light from the flash, her face was a mask of pain.

She leaned away from him. He could hear the rustling of fabric as she pulled the strap of her nightgown back up to her shoulders. In the darkness, he imagined that she faced away from him as she reached down and pulled the bedcovers up to her chin.

Forte stepped over to a loveseat and sat on the edge of it. "You are a beautiful woman…"

"Hush," she said. Her voice was soft but insistent. "My fault."

Outside the wind howled and the rain pummeled the windows.

She reached over to the bedside and turned on the radio. A slow-dance tune from Duke Ellington filled the room. She reached into the drawer under the table and pulled out cigarettes and a lighter. She lit one without offering one to him. In the light of the flame, he could see her tear-streaked cheeks. "Tyson wouldn't let me smoke in here," she said.

He did not respond. In the darkness of the room, he could smell the smoke before he saw it. It held no comfort for him.

"You were dreaming," he said.

She inhaled and held it. He could tell from the cigarette's glow that her face was still pointed away from him. "I don't remember."

"You screamed."

The red tip of the cigarette pointed at him. "I did?"

"Yes. It's why I came in here."

"Oh," she said.

He stood up. His head felt light. "The pain comes out in different ways sometimes." He moved toward the door.

She said nothing at first. When she spoke, her voice was so soft he could barely hear her now. "I'm sorry."

He paused, his hand on the door. "Yeah, me too."

He closed the door behind him and walked to the rail overlooking the den. He stood with his hands on the rail looking at the darkness below for a moment. Then he turned and walked to the landing and down the stairs.

On the second floor landing he glanced at Hallee's closed door as he started down the stairs.

He stopped.

Hallee's door was closed.

Closed? Hadn't he left it open earlier?

He raced toward Hallee's room and crashed open the door.

The bed was empty.

# Chapter 14

*Sunday, 3 a.m.*

Three eight-foot yellow ladders straddled the furniture in the den, FBI technicians perched atop them. They busily plucked screwdrivers from their tool belts as they dismantled the sconce light fixtures on the wall and the battery-operated fire alarm. Another technician stood in front of the security system box by the kitchen door, peering into the tangle of wires inside the defaced unit. The white carpet in the den was waffled with muddy footprints.

Forte sat in an easy chair near the corner where he had set up his watch post, watching the army of people rushing in and out of the house. On the dining room table rested his shotgun, its shells pocketed by the first cop on the scene. Forte had been running through the Garden District away from the house when two New Orleans police cars caught up with him, took away his weapon and made him lie on the street face-down. He could still feel bits of street grit on the front of his black tee-shirt. When Rosalind Dent had shown up a quarter hour later, he was uncuffed, interviewed briefly by one of her assistants, and told to remain at the house but stay out of the way.

If anyone in the house happened to look in his direction, they saw a disheveled man with a comatose expression on his face. Underneath, Forte seethed. But he forced himself into a state of numbness. He would let the strong emotions come to him later. For the moment, however, he listened, straining to pick up every bit of information he could.

A man in a suit with a clipboard spoke quietly to the technician at the alarm panel. "A remote device?"

The technician illuminated the inside of the alarm box with a small flashlight. "Yep. Look. Here's where the override unit was clipped into the system. It was really small and hidden behind the wires. You wouldn't have noticed it at first even if you were looking for something hinky in here. When he wanted to shut off the system, he just hit a button on his remote. When he wanted to turn the alarms back on, he hit another button."

Another tech with a beard joined them, holding up a small electronic component in his rubber-gloved hand. "Found six of these miniature cameras so far. The newest and best. These little babies can capture high-resolution video images in low-light and beam them a mile away. Sweet."

The man in the suit jotted notes on the clipboard, glanced at Forte then motioned to the others to move to another room.

Rosalind Dent came through the front door wearing an FBI raincoat with the hood laid back on her shoulders. Her short-cropped black hair was spiked with moisture. She walked past Forte without looking at him. Another agent in a suit waited for her at the bottom of the stairs while he scraped mud off his shoes with the edge of a clipboard.

"No blood in the girl's bedroom. No signs of struggle," he said, his voice low. "The lab needs to confirm, but looks like he drugged her, took her out the window, lowered her down from the garage roof, took her over the wall and through the neighbor's yard.

Neighbor's dog was found knocked out." He looked up from the notebook in his hand. "The guy is strong and knows what the hell he's doing."

Rosalind Dent listened to the man, patted him on the shoulder and murmured something Forte could not hear. She turned and walked over to him and sat in the chair he had first brought from the dining room for his night watch.

"You okay?" she said.

He did not look at her, keeping his gaze straight ahead.

Dent sighed. "Yeah, dumb question." She unbuttoned the raincoat, stood up and took it off and laid it on the floor next to the chair. She sat down again.

"Listen," she said, "I probably don't need to tell you this, but you are off this case. From what we can tell, you had the deck stacked against you here. The kidnapper could see every move you made. But the word has come down from above that you don't have access to this situation any more. I'm sorry, Al." She brushed the water from her hair with her fingertips "You can collect your weapon. The shotgun shells are with a cop in the study." She stood up.

Forte held up his hand. "And what about Mrs. Lamberth?"

"Upstairs with a doctor. Screamed herself mute. Doc gave her something to knock her out."

Forte nodded. "Thanks, Rosie."

She touched his shoulder and walked away.

He stood up and walked into the dining room. He picked up the shotgun, checked the safety and walked down the hallway to the first-floor study. A young woman in an FBI jacket sat at a computer, scrolling through files. A cop looked over her shoulder.

As Forte approached the cop to ask about his shells, the computer speakers emitted a voice message in a soft female voice, "You have mail."

The FBI tech double-clicked on the e-mail icon and a window popped up on the screen. Forte stepped closer, scanning the monitor quickly. The message read:

```
Hallee is safe for now.
My demand is simple: if you want to see
Hallee again have $25 million ready to be
wired to an off-shore account by 5 p.m.
Monday. That deadline is non-negotiable.
I will contact you before then with
details for the transfer of the money and
for a meeting place where you can recover
Hallee.
Please do not make me prove even further
that I am serious about my intentions.
For proof of authenticity that I
actually have Hallee, look on the collar of
her stuffed tiger.
For the child's sake, comply with my
demands.
                The Rescuer
```

Forte backed away from the desk and the FBI tech rushed past him, looking for Dent, the agent-in-charge. Another tech pointed to the kitchen door and the computer tech sprinted toward the door followed by the cop who had been in the study with her.

Forte stepped back to the computer and checked the mail account settings in the e-mail program. He jotted some notes quickly then closed the menu and left the e-mail message on the screen exactly like the FBI tech had left it.

He walked up the stairs and went into Hallee's room. He could hear noises from the bathroom but the bedroom was empty. He walked to the window seat where the stuffed tiger lay on its back. On the collar was a small medal. Forte bent and read the words etched on it: Proverbs 24:11.

He quickly turned and walked out of the room and down the stairs. He leaned against the wall in the hallway as a group of FBI agents ran past him and up the stairs.

He poked his head inside the study where the cop still stood. "Got my shells?" he asked.

The cop nodded and fished a clear plastic bag out of his jacket with seven shotgun shells in it. Forte took the bag and thanked the cop.

Outside the study in the hallway, he nearly bumped into a figure standing next to the door. It was Tolan.

"Guess you did the best you could," the NCLU man said. "Or is that insensitive of me to say?"

Forte said nothing. He moved to go around Tolan but the man put a hand on his arm.

"Forte, I don't know what you were doing in Mrs. Lamberth's room last night, but I hope it doesn't result in any more harm to this family."

Forte took the man's fingers and bent them away from his arm. He looked at Tolan's bulldog face but did not respond. There was nothing to say.

Tolan glared at him a moment longer then walked away.

# Chapter 15

*Sunday, 4 a.m.*

Forte held the whiskey bottle above his head, gripping it tightly by the neck with his sparring-gloved hand as he tried to read the label in the darkness of the balcony. In the sky above the balcony, the storm had cleared but the moon still hid behind some clouds.

The bottle was still sealed. Larue had given the whiskey to him at his high school graduation. Two days later he shipped out with the Navy. Much later, when Forte had submitted himself to the drug treatment program, he had kept several boxes in storage while he sorted out his life. When The Refuge was founded, he had rediscovered the bottle. It had remained, unopened, on a shelf in the closet of his guest bedroom.

He had gone straight to the workout room when he left the Lamberth home. The guards who had just finished working out had stayed for a few minutes while he pounded the heavy bag. Whumpf. Whumpf. Left. Right. His anger was the first emotion to be dealt with and this was the safest way to do it. Whumpf. So damn stupid. Whumpf, whumpf. So completely careless. So... whumpf... totally... whumpf... irresponsible... whumpf, whumpf, whumpf. So totally irresponsible. He punched out his anger until he could no longer bring up his arms from his sides.

Now he sat on his balcony, slumped in the round thick cushion of the cane lounge chair in the corner. The anger was gone now and he was left with the guilt and the misery of having failed at his mission. He missed the anger already.

He pressed the whiskey bottle against the sweat of his forehead. The glass felt cool.

Just one drink to take the edge off, to soothe him.

Just one.

He tilted the bottle and looked at it from every angle. The gold and red seal still intact, covering the cap at the top. The neck sloping gracefully down to the body where the insignia for the liquor company stood out in beautiful clear raised ridges on the sturdy glass.

Just one drink would give him enough courage to make that short walk down the street to any corner where any one of a handful of street entrepreneurs could make his pain go away in ten minutes.

One drink. Ten minutes.

'Til paradise.

Then, more pain.

He leaned forward. The clouds uncovered a sliver of moon. He held the bottle between his knees and looked at it. A single tear dropped and hit the neck of the bottle. He watched it slowly move down the glass. He set the bottle on the floor next to the chair.

He would have to deal with the pain now. As it came to him.

He leaned back and sank into the cushion and put a hand over his eyes. As soon as his eyes closed, he saw the empty bed, as he knew he would. He saw wet ends of the curtains whipping away from the open window as he dove through it onto the roof, rolling to the edge and dropping to the ground below and hurtling through the wetness following the footprints to the broken bush in the corner of the yard next to the brick wall with the streaks of dirt where boots had clambered over, then over he went and through the next yard with the house lights coming on upstairs and through the open gate and down the driveway out on the street where nothing moved and down the street gasping and around the corner to the next street and the next and the next as he ran blindly through the rain.

Then the rain was gone and he was on another street in another time and place, a street more narrow and bordered by buildings instead of trees. Around the corner. A woman lying in the alley grime clutching red at her chest. A boy running past, eyes white-wild with fear. His wife, in his arms, the blood soaking his front, her eyes on his face until the light behind them flickered low and died out. The pain coming up from the deep, refusing to be covered up, refusing to be ignored, insisting on boiling to the surface where it could wrack with sobs that no person should hear. Or feel. *Ruth, Ruth, too late... too late...*

He jerked awake, his arms poised in mid-reach in the air in front of him. His face was wet.

Boo sat perfectly still on the balcony rail, watching him but not coming near.

Forte picked up the cordless phone next to the chair. He cleared his throat and hit the speed-dial button labeled number one.

Manning Laird picked up on the first ring. His Bronx-accented voice sounded strong and clear. "Manny here."

"Do you ever sleep?" Forte said.

"Almost as much as you do," Manny said. In the background, a teapot began the first hollow strains of a whistle. "Somehow I have come to believe that sleep is a highly overrated commodity."

Forte held the phone against his ear. On the other end there was a comfortable silence.

"Here's the thing," Forte said. He told about the kidnapping.

Manny said nothing on the other end until he had finished. "A time of danger for you."

"Yes, it was."

"I mean now."

"I know what you meant," Forte said.

Manny let silence fill the phone line between them. For all his glibness, he was unafraid of a still moment between friends.

Forte listened to his friend's even breathing. "Isn't this where the sponsor is supposed to talk the addict out of roaming the streets to score some dope?"

"Nah," said Manny. "That's just in the movies."

Forte smiled in the darkness. Boo leaped down from the rail and into his lap.

Manny spoke. "So, what are you going to do?"

Forte stroked Boo's head between the ears. "First, I'm going to sit here in awe of your marvelous therapeutic style."

"Yeah, I get that a lot. And after that, what?"

"After that … nothing. I take the next step in living a real life, crappy as it may be."

Manny was silent for a beat on the other end. The whistling of the kettle had stopped. "Yes," he said, "I believe you will."

Forte dragged the back of his hand across his cheek. "Thanks, Manny."

"Come see me later on today," Manny said, then hung up.

Forte pressed the button to disconnect and let the cordless phone hang from his fingers next to the chair. He felt the floor touch the bottom of the phone and he let it go.

Boo got up and stretched, then circled once and lay down on his lap again. Forte closed his eyes. This time, no demons. Just darkness for a while.

# Chapter 16

*Sunday, 11:25 a.m.*

The organ swelled on cue as the choir director flourished his baton, bringing in the orchestra for a final crescendo as it joined with the voices of dozens of  singers robed in purple and gold. Three television cameras caught the performance from three different viewpoints in the sanctuary: close-up, mid-way from the back, and high-angle from the balcony where the sun splashed through windows stained in abstract hues.

Forte sat in the back near the center door wearing black chino pants, black boots, and his best white silk tee-shirt. His black leather jacket was draped over the back of the pew. No one had spoken to him since he entered the church except for one of the greeters in the lobby who had put a church bulletin in his hand before looking at his face. "Welcome... uh, friend," the man said, his greeter's special smile locked in place but his eyes showing confusion. Now as Forte sat on the pew, several of the people around him glanced at him from the corners of their eyes as they reached for a hymnal or adjusted a cufflink or pretended to search for a friend's face across the aisle. A blond-haired girl, maybe four years old, peeked over the back of the pew in front of him. An attractive woman next to the girl pulled the child down to the cushioned bench without turning to look behind her.

Forte picked up a Bible on the pew next to him, looked up Proverbs in the index  and turned to Proverbs 24:11-12. It read: "If thou forbear to deliver them that are drawn unto death, and those that are ready to be slain; If thou sayest, Behold, we knew it not; doth not he that pondereth the heart consider it? and he that keepeth thy soul, doth not he know it? and shall not he render to every man according to his works?"

The choir anthem had ended. A man strode to the center of the carpeted stage that was surrounded on three sides by pews fanning out and packed with people. Even from the back of  the cavernous room, Forte could recognize him as the pastor, Jason Hamilton, from the man's web pages that he had printed out before catching the flight to Houston earlier.

Forte had awakened to a sun-drenched Sunday morning, the only time of the week that the Quarter approached a period of quietness. He had showered, made a few phone calls,  then checked the Internet for news about the kidnapping. It was there as the lead story on CNN.COM. "Daughter of Murdered Abortion Doctor Missing." A smiling head-and-shoulder photo of Hallee in a spangle-covered dance outfit was next to the headline on the web page. He saw his name in the third paragraph of the story as he scanned down,  but he didn't stop to read it. Didn't matter, what's done is done. He had searched for and found Jason Hamilton's web page and printed out a half-dozen pages outlining the group's crusade "to battle wickedness everywhere in order to advance the kingdom of God."

None of Forte's contacts would have much for him until later in the day. So when there's nothing else you can do, he had told himself, do something anyway. He had driven to the airport and barely had time for coffee, a bagel, and Checkers number one before catching the flight to Houston.

Now he was listening to the man himself. Hamilton had taken a medium-sized Houston church and in seven years had increased its size twenty-fold by striding back and forth across the stage and insisting in his booming voice that the Lord would bless those who opposed evil, specifically the kind of evil espoused by abortionists and homosexuals. Hamilton had led dozens of protests across the nation, his followers holding signs proclaiming "The Lord Hates Faggots" and "God will kill baby-killers," depending on the type of event he had targeted. The more the so-called liberal media had lambasted his point of view, the more popular he had become and the bigger his church had grown.

Hamilton stood at the pulpit and looked out over his congregation for a moment before speaking. He raised his hand. "Hallelujah!" he bellowed.

The crowd echoed him. "Hallelujah!"

"Today," Hamilton intoned, "before I bring the word of the Lord to you, I want us to pause in prayer for the kidnapped child of the abortionist Dr. Tyson Lamberth. Although her father is even now roasting in the never-ending flames of Hell for the wickedness he propagated here on Earth, his daughter Hallee Lamberth does not deserve the fear and possible death that may come her way simply because she is a member of a family where no righteousness reigned. She does not deserve fear any more than the millions of babies who have perished under the blades of abortionists right here in America since our country said it was lawful to kill those tiny children while in their mother's wombs ..." Hamilton continued in his prayer, then launched into a sermon that stretched out for the next 40 minutes.

Forte glanced around him and could find no one who was not paying rapt attention to Hamilton's sermon. He sat quietly and waited.

At the end of the service, the choir segued into a praise chorus that the congregation apparently knew by heart because everyone joined in. Hamilton stretched out his hands and proclaimed a benediction before striding down the stage to a side door.

Forte watched him go, then stood up and made his away against the flood of people moving toward the exits at the back of the church. People looked at him more openly now.

Finally, he reached the doors at the front of the sanctuary and walked down a passageway until he came to a sign above a door: Church Offices. He opened the door and walked through a large reception area with two modern-looking workdesks and a more traditional receptionist's desk in the center of the room. He walked down a hallway to a door with an engraved sign that read "Pastor's Office." He opened the door. Almost immediately he felt the muzzle of a hand-gun pressed against his temple.

"Freeze!" the man holding the gun yelled. Forte froze. "Hands over your head!"

Forte slowly raised his hands.

Across the room sat Pastor Hamilton behind a boat of a desk. He had raised a bottle of Perrier to drink. His tie was loosened and his face was twisted into an expression that looked like a mix of shock and fear. When he saw that the danger had passed, his face relaxed. "Barry," he said to the man holding the gun, "son, you need to remember to lock that office door. This boy coulda done killed us both if he wanted to." He waved Barry to put down the gun and looked at Forte. "Please pardon Barry's response to your rather abrupt appearance here today, Mr. Forte. We get some threats from time to time and have to be on our guard a bit. And just what brings you to our little church meeting today, Mr. Forte?"

Forte put his hands down and looked at the man with the gun. Barry looked like a model for a young Aryan's bodybuilder magazine: blond hair cut stylishly short, blue eyes, tan suit with tiny blue pinstripes. He slid a .44 magnum revolver back into a holster under his suit jacket, carefully buttoned the coat, and took three steps away from Forte, still eyeing him as he stood at parade rest.

Forte looked at Hamilton. "You know me?"

Hamilton grinned. "Why, Mr. Forte, you look just like your picture on CNN this mornin'. I must've had a half-dozen phone calls before church about your mishap over in New Orleans." He stopped smiling. "I repeat, why are you here, Mr. Forte?"

Forte walked over and sat down in one of the chairs in front of the pastor's desk. The oak desk and two matching guest chairs rested on an oriental rug that covered a third of the office. A ponderous conference table surrounded by ten chairs occupied another third of the office. It was separated from Hamilton's work area by a seating area with a leather sofa and two leather easy chairs. On the wall behind the pastor's desk was a six-foot framed painting that depicted Moses coming down from the mountain with the tablets. Over the painting in elaborate silver scroll were the Ten Commandments.

"I think you may be able to help me," he said to Hamilton.

"And why should I?" the pastor said.

"Because of the girl."

"That is unfortunate. It is really."

"But you don't have any idea who is behind this?"

"Behind what – the murder of the abortionist or the kidnapping of his daughter?"

"Both. The same people probably did both. Too much of a coincidence."

A phone rang in the outer office. Forte could see a light flashing on the phone on the pastor's credenza. Hamilton didn't pick it up.

"We talked to the FBI yesterday morning, right after Dr. Lamberth came to his deserved end," said Hamilton. "I don't believe we can shed any further light on the kidnapping of the Lamberth girl, as much as I would like to."

"You are lying."

Hamilton's face colored. "Could be, Mr. Forte," the pastor said, "but you are a guest here, and I advise you to mind your tongue before Barry teaches you some manners."

"Barry does look like a well-mannered lad, I agree," Forte said, "but good manners don't always win the day, now do they? Otherwise, all your hate-mongering would never have given you such a nice office and a suit that cost as much as some people's cars."

Hamilton laughed. "Hate-mongering? Tsk, tsk, Mr. Forte. You haven't been reading your Bible lately, have you? The evil that I oppose is the same evil that God has always opposed. I didn't make it up. God did. He said that homosexuals should be put to death. Now, we just carry signs and call for changes in our country's laws to put an end to the perversion all around us. That's not much, is it, compared to ... death? Besides, are you going to sit there and tell me you think it was fine and dandy for Dr. Lamberth to be killing all those unborn babies all these years?"

Forte kept quiet.

Hamilton pointed a finger at him. "Deep down you agree with me, I know it."

More silence from Forte.

"He deserved to die way before he did," Hamilton said.

"According to you as judge and jury."

"According to any measure of decency."

"And you know who did it, don't you?"

Hamilton glared at him. "No."

"But you know some people who probably could have done it?"

"You are sounding like the FBI now, Mr. Forte, and I'm afraid that is not a favorable comparison." The pastor tilted his chair back and put his wing-tips on the corner of the desk. "But I will answer your question because, even though you are a traitor to any belief in God you may have possessed at one time, I think you are trying to do the right thing by finding the girl." His face had softened. "God moves in mysterious ways, and He could allow the girl to die. But she is innocent and I believe in protecting the innocent." He paused. "Our methods and talents are different, but we are more alike in our mission than you will admit."

"I doubt that," Forte said. "But, back to my question. You might have known who did this thing?"

Hamilton motioned to Barry to shut the office door. To Forte he said, "I will tell you this, and it is more than I told the FBI people. I spent nearly two hours this morning checking out the whereabouts of anyone I think could have done it. The handful of people who are out of pocket at the moment... they would certainly possess the ability and conviction to kill the doctor if they chose to do so. But they would not be the type of people who would kidnap the girl.

"Mr. Forte, you may disagree with my message and my tactics. But there are lines we would not cross to justify our ends."

Forte searched the pastor's face. "And those people, who are out of pocket... if I came up with proof that any one of them could have stolen the girl...?"

Hamilton stood up. "I would help you find him."

Forte came to his feet. "Good." He held out his hand and Hamilton shook it.

# Chapter 17

*Sunday, 3 p.m.*

Café Du Monde was always filled with tourists in springtime, but Forte still braved the crowds from time to time. Somehow, amid all the hubbub, his mind could disconnect here.

The weekend visitors -- families with kids clutching balloon giraffes and couples wrapped up in honeymoons – had mostly left the city by this hour on Sunday afternoon. But the conventioneers and business people with meetings the next morning had taken their place. Forte sat in the corner of the outside courtyard next to a table of four young women with nametags on the lapels of their suits. They had been stealing glances at him as he sipped his café au lait behind his darkest shades. One of them, a blonde who looked like she had just stepped off the sidelines and exchanged her cheerleader outfit for a business suit, got up and scooted her chair over to his table.

"Would you mind taking our picture," she said, holding out a yellow throwaway camera. Her nametag read "Denise Brazier, National Women Trial Lawyers Association."

Forte turned to look at her for a moment, then took the camera without saying anything and looked through the viewfinder at the women who huddled together and flashed their best smiles. Two of the women had big diamond engagement rings on their hands. He snapped the picture and tossed the camera back to the blonde.

"Thanks," she said. "We were about to go for a Hurricane. Could you tell us where Pat O'Brien's is?" The other three women were casually watching him over their heavy coffee mugs. A cartoon image popped into his head: Tweety Bird in his cage, surrounded by cats.

He pointed toward the corner of Jackson Square. "It's on St. Peter. Just walk along the far side of the Square and keep going. Pat O'Brien's is on the left. Can't miss it." None of the women followed with their eyes the direction of his pointing finger, their attention still on his sunglasses. Why do people think you can't see them looking at you when you are wearing shades, Forte wondered.

"Thanks again," the blonde said. "Care to join us?" One of the women, thin and dark-skinned with a model's cheekbones, put a hand over her mouth to hide a giggle.

"Bet you've already been there this afternoon," he said. All the women laughed now.

"Could be," their spokesperson said. "But we didn't have a guide then."

"I appreciate the offer," he said, "But, sorry, can't help you."

The blonde groaned and the thin woman slapped the table. "Pay up," she said. The other three brought their purses up to the table, rummaged through them and took out $20 bills which the black woman folded together and put in her suit pocket. "Come to mama," she said as she looked up at the blonde. "Losing your touch, Denise?"

Denise stood up and looped her purse strap over her shoulder. "The day's still young," she said, bringing another gale of laughter from her pals. The others stood up, waggled their fingers in a goodbye wave to Forte, then gathered their purses and wended their way through the tables out to the street. Their high heels clicked out a syncopated beat that almost blended with the Dixieland jazz band on the corner.

Denise stopped and touched his shoulder. "Not even tempted?"

Forte looked at her. "I'm not dead. Just numb at the moment." Her touch felt warm on his shoulder. "What was the bet?"

She smiled and waved a finger in front of his face. "You'd only get to know that if I won the bet. Hope you get un-numbed sometime," she said. She smiled and walked away.

Forte watched her catch up with her friends. The group crossed the street and meandered past the sketch artists, palm readers and street performers on the wide sidewalk in front of Jackson Square. They skirted around one of the horse-drawn carriages and went through the front gate of the black wrought-iron fence surrounding the square.

He had called Jon Brach from a pay phone at the airport just before having a cab bring him directly to the Café Du Monde. Forte had been blocked from the investigation of the kidnapping, but his reporter friend would have updated information. The pay phone would provide a bit more security than the cell phone in his pocket. As his Navy SEAL commander had once said: Better to be paranoid than sorry. The call had been fairly fruitless though. Brach said the e-mailed ransom note had been forwarded through four anonymous e-mail addresses and was untraceable so far.

Before he had left for Houston, Forte had placed several phone calls to contacts in the intelligence community and ex-Special Forces men on his special mission contact list. The work that needed to be done on this case was different from a regular mission where a client hired Forte to recover a child. In those cases, some level of cooperation was established by the law enforcement officials also working the case. With his involvement in Hallee's case – after having been banned from it – he would have to take another approach. But, as one of his commando squad members from Tennessee always said, "Ain't no hill for a stepper."

He pulled his cell phone out of his pocket. This was a call he had to make but did not relish. He punched in a number and listened. On the other end, at the Lamberth home, an FBI agent picked up. "Please keep this line clear," the tech said in a curt tone. His cell phone number and name had obviously popped up on the caller ID.

"Wait, don't disconnect," Forte said. "Is Agent Dent there?"

There was silence on the line then Rosalind Dent picked up. "Al, we are monitoring this line for a possible call from the kidnapper."

"Rosie, I just need to say one thing to Mrs. Lamberth," he said.

Rosie said nothing for a beat, then, "Hold on."

Forte let his eyes roam over the thinning crowd across the street. A bum in a wool knit cap walked toward the gate of the Square, a half-dozen plastic grocery bags dangling from his arms.

Freida Lamberth came on the line. "Hello?" Her voice was tremulous.

"Mrs. Lamberth, this is Al Forte. We didn't get to talk after what happened last night." He stopped and listened. He could hear her breathing. "I wanted to hear it from you directly though. Do you want me off this case? Yes or no."

On the other end, the woman gave a small gasp. "I think that would be best, yes, Mr. Forte." Her voice faltered as she said his name.

Forte paused, then continued. "I'm sorry. I let you down." He knew every word was being heard by at least two agents and recorded by the FBI.

"Yes," she said. "Me too." The line went dead.

Forte folded the phone and put it back in his pocket. As you wish. But he would do what he had to do.

He picked up a beignet and shook it twice over the plate to knock off the excess powdered sugar. He took a healthy bite of the french donut and washed it down with the coffee. As he ate he watched the bum with the shopping bags walk away from him down St. Ann. The man tipped open the swinging lid of a garbage can and peered in. Most people walking along the pedestrian-only street ignored him.

As Forte watched the bum, his eyes refocused on another figure walking toward him, about 60 yards beyond the garbage can where the bum had stopped. Poochie, wearing a gray silk suit and white crew neck shirt, ambled toward him, a polished black oak cane swinging at his side. He tapped the ground with the cane about every third step. Forte felt a tingle on the back of his neck.

Slowly Forte turned his head and searched the milling crowds up and down Decatur Street from behind his shades. He stretched and glanced up and behind him along the Moonwalk that bordered the river and ran atop the levee next to the café. He saw no sign of Poochie's henchmen or anyone else who seemed to be taking any special notice of him.

The drug dealer strolled up to the corner and stopped to listen to the jazz band. Two trombone players were in the middle of trading improv licks in "Won't You Come Home, Bill Bailey." A bass, guitar, trumpet, snare drum and clarinet rounded out the band. Poochie stood with one foot slightly ahead of the other, swaying slightly while tapping the cane in time to the music. The tune came to an end and he pulled a roll of bills out of his pocket, peeled off three bills  and dropped them in the five-gallon white plastic bucket in front of the jazz players. He walked across the street to the café.

Forte casually scratched his lower back, pulled the Glock nine-millimeter automatic from the holster, turned off the safety and held the gun against his leg as the other man approached his table.

"Well, well, Al-veeeen," said the drug dealer, his yellow-brown face lit up in a dazzling smile. "Mind if I have a seat?" He sat without waiting for an answer and hooked the cane over the back of the chair.

"What can I do for you, Poochie?" Forte said. From behind the shades, his eyes continued to search the background for signs of a setup.

The other man smiled more broadly now. "Al, what up with your manners, sonny boy? How about 'Poochie, so good to see you' or 'Poochie, how about a cup o' coffee?' or 'Poochie, thanks for your help yesterday.'"

Forte did not respond, his hand still on the gun.

Poochie held up his hands, his bejeweled fingers splayed in front of him. "Al-righty, I can understand you being in a bad mood, seeing what you been through recently." He almost sang the last part of the sentence, the way preachers sometimes do when mimicking someone. Ree-cent-LEEEE.

One of the café's Vietnamese waitresses stopped at the table and the drug dealer ordered a coffee. She shot a glance at the gun next to Forte's leg, her face unchanging. She scurried away to take another order. Poochie leaned back in the chair and took a deep breath. Across the street the jazz band was packing up to make room for the next street performer. "That Squirrel, he can handle a gun now, can't he?"

"Squirrel?"

"Yeah, the white boy with the goatee who saved your Navy SEAL hiney yesterday. He's a little crazy, you know, squirrelly. But he sho can shoot." He waved a hand as if he were erasing a blackboard. "But that ain't why I'm here. Forget that."

The waitress came back with a tray loaded with coffee mugs. She set one in front of the small man and kept moving. Poochie took a sip and said, "Ahhhhhh. Nothing like it." He took out a silver cigarette case and flipped open the lid. He held it out to Forte, who shook his head. He pulled out a long thin brown cigarette, lit it and inhaled deeply.

Forte picked up his coffee mug with his left hand and drank, keeping his right hand on the gun under the table. "Poochie, you did not come here to drink coffee and chat. And if you are here to talk about getting Kyra back, the answer is still no."

The man held up the hand with the cigarette between two fingers, a crooked ribbon of smoke trailing from the lit end. "Now Alveeeeen, you might be changing your mind when you hear what I have to say."

"I'm listening."

"What if I told you I might know something about the guy who killed the doctor."

Forte's eyebrows rose above the shades. "Keep talking."

"Well, just suppose I did know something about him. We could trade for that kind of information, couldn't we now, Al?"

"What do you have in mind?"

"Kyra. Give her to me. We can keep her safe until we take care of the Colombians."

Forte lifted his coffee mug and drained it. Oh for an uncloudy day. He moved the pistol back to its holster. "Even if I wanted to do that, you know the DEA's office would close us down. They assigned Kyra to the Refuge until their investigation is over."

Poochie suddenly slammed his fist down on the table, causing shock tremors in the surface of the coffee in the mugs. A pair of businessmen at the next table jumped at the sound, one of them cursing as he spilled coffee on his jacket.

"Dammit, Forte," Poochie said, his voice rasping as he leaned forward and whispered. "I'm trying to help you here. That other girl, the white girl, she could die. And you sit here talking about investigations."

Forte took off his sunglasses and leaned forward, his mouth a hard thin line. "Listen, don't talk to me about people dying or you trying to help. I'd hate like hell if the girl died. But I'm not going to release Kyra to you. She's as safe or safer with us than with you. So, if you want to help me, give me your information. If not, then get the hell away from me."

The two men sat glaring at each other. At the next table, the pair of businessmen got up and moved to the other side of the courtyard. A lone saxophonist started up with "What a Wonderful World" on the corner. It wasn't Louie but it was something, Forte thought.

Poochie settled back in his chair and crossed his arms as he looked across the street toward General Jackson tipping his hat.

"A visit then," he said.

"A visit?"

"Me... with Kyra."

"At The Refuge?"

Poochie nodded. Forte leaned back and said nothing. The horn player was wrapping up the song. The dozen or so people who had stopped to listen gave him a smattering of applause. Half the people stooped and put bills in the man's hat before walking away.

"I think I can swing that," Forte said.

"Good," Poochie said. He pulled out a cell phone, hit a speed-dial button, waited for the connection and spoke three words into the phone, then hung up. "A good friend of mine, someone who depends on me muchly, says he did a little work for the man a while back. Some ID work. He will talk to you about it, as a favor to me, but he won't talk to the cops. He's got to be protected." Poochie looked at his watch. "But if we gonna see him, it better be soon 'cause he's overdue for a bit of happiness in his life at the moment."

"I don't want to see any substance being passed," Forte said. "You know the drill on that."

Poochie grinned. "No prob, Alveen."

A silver Mercedes sports utility vehicle pulled up to the curb. The drug dealer jerked his head toward it. "Let's go," he said.

Forte looked at the truck. "I thought you guys drove Cadillacs."

Poochie stood up and retrieved his cane from the back of the chair.

"Gotta keep up with the Joneses," he said.

# Chapter 18

*Sunday, 3:20 p.m.*

The blindfold cut into his cheeks a little, but Forte figured he wouldn't be wearing it for very long. He could feel the truck taking quick lefts and rights without traveling along a straightaway for any length of time. In the enclosed cab of the SUV, the Skull Cap's cologne hung heavy.

The truck stopped and Forte was helped down to a sidewalk. He could hear an iron gate swinging open and clanging to a stop. A large hand on his biceps guided him forward about 20 yards. From the way his footsteps echoed so closely around him, he felt he must be walking down a very small alleyway. He bumped into Skull Cap and could feel a large revolver under the man's coat. It was like bumping into a wall. Then he was out walking in a more open space. Beneath his feet he could feel the uneven bricks of a courtyard. On the skin on his face he could feel the slight breeze of outside air compared to the stillness of the interior of a building.

Another door opened and the group stepped into an apartment. Incense blanketed the room, stronger than the cologne smell in the truck but not strong enough to cover the aroma of marijuana. Forte felt a little dizzy. "Let's get this over with quick," he said.

Fingers tugged at his blindfold. It came free. They were standing in a den decorated with a pin-striped sofa and two European-style contemporary chairs. A two-foot-high stack of  electronics and computer graphics magazines leaned precariously next to an octagon coffee table made of  a tile mosaic. A signed Blue Dog print that looked like an original hung on the fashionably cracked plaster wall behind the couch. Skull Cap was standing a hand-span away from Forte, glaring down at him. Poochie stood near the entrance to a hallway, next to a gangly man with stringy pale brown hair. "Benny gonna show you his stuff. This way," Poochie said.

Down the hallway were two doors. One was shut. The other led into an office setup with a wraparound workstation that covered two of the walls. A 21-inch monitor glowed in the corner of the workstation. On a shelf above the monitor was a high-end scanner. The computer box that controlled the components hummed away on the floor under the desk. On the shelves above the workstation were piles of electronic gadgets and components. In the opposite corner of the room a digital camera on a tripod faced a chair in front of a dark blue pull-down background shade. Somewhere in the jumble a police scanner squawked with a dispatch to a domestic violence situation out in Chalmette.

"Show and tell, Benny," Poochie said.

Benny was standing by the rolling chair, his hand twitching as he tugged at his earlobe. His eyes never left Poochie. He sat at the desk and clicked the mouse until Adobe PhotoShop opened on the screen. He clicked some more and three small photos appeared. He enlarged them. "Dude came here about seven months ago, needing some ID." He pointed to the middle photo on the screen. "This is how he looked." The picture showed a sharp-faced man with blue eyes and short spiked blond hair.

"He had some rough drawings of how he wanted the other two photos to look. I had to doctor them a good bit. He came back twice to check them before he was satisfied. Then I made the papers for him.." He paused and tapped the picture on the left side of the screen. "This is how I recognized it was the guy." The picture showed a man with long black hair and eyebrows, dark eyes and a black beard. "I also lined up two cell phones for him, each with a year's prepaid service. Untraceable." He rotated his chair slowly to face the room. "Nobody can know I gave you this information. I wouldn't get a nickel's worth of business if people thought I would give them up."

"Why are you giving this guy up?" Forte asked, knowing it was a cruel question. He regretted asking it as soon as he saw the desperate expression on the counterfeiter's face.

"Because Poochie asked me to do it," Benny said, his head bowed.

Forte felt suddenly tired. "Give me the names and addresses for all of the ID's." Benny whirled the chair around to the computer and clicked a few more times. After about ten seconds, the laser printer at the end of the desk whirred and the documents printed out.

Forte looked at them. He took out his wallet and removed a business card from it. Turning it over, he put it on the desktop, leaned over and wrote something. He handed the card to Benny. "Thanks."

Benny took it. "Oh, one more thing. The guy didn't seem like someone who would ordinarily be doing this, setting up other identities. I mean, I can't put my finger on it. But it was like .... he acted almost like he was a cop. First time he came here, I thought he was going to bust me. The way he looked over the place, like he was looking for something to bust me for."

Forte thought about that but said nothing.

Poochie nodded at Skull Cap. "Put the blindfold back on him and wait for me in the car." Forte closed his eyes and felt the black cloth tighten around his head a bit more than necessary. He was guided back to the truck.

Ten minutes later, the front passenger door opened and slammed shut. "Let's roll," Poochie said.

Forte had the sensation that he was being watched by the drug dealer in the front seat. "I saw what you gave Benny," Poochie said. He cursed softly, disgust in his voice. "You think he is gonna fold up his business, his life, and go to a treatment center?"

"It's no life now, what Benny is living. He only thinks it is," Forte said. His own voice sounded louder than usual to him.

"And you know better than he does how to run his life."

"I know a junkie when I see one. Been there, done that, burned the tee-shirt."

"Maybe he can handle it better than you."

"Right. We wouldn't have been there today if he could handle it." Forte felt his anger rising. "Nobody can handle it."

He heard the drug dealer sigh. "Preach it, brother."

Forte forced himself to count to ten under his breath. "Poochie, if you had to sit and talk to every mother whose child has lost everything to dope – his job, his family, sometimes even his life – you would put yourself out of your own misery, fast."

Poochie said nothing for a long moment. "Enough talk, Forte. Our deal didn't include you preaching to me." He muttered something to his driver. Forte could only hear "… damn ex-junkies think they…"

Forte was mute, thankful that he didn't have to see Poochie at the moment. The worse thing was, the man was right. He had no right to tell anyone else what to do. As a good friend of his had once said: Everybody gotta learn from their own mistakes.

He slumped against the door and waited for the ride to end.

\* \* \*

The small girl had set up the miniature table and chairs in a corner of the courtyard, as far from the sand box as she could get. "We no want to get sand in our tea, now do we?" She stood over the table with a plastic pitcher and carefully poured imaginary liquid into the tea cups on the table for her guest.

The man, knees poking above each side of the tiny table as he shifted in the small chair, picked up the cup and gingerly held it up close to his mouth. He tilted his head back, eyes closed in play ecstasy, then set the cup on the table and rubbed his stomach in a circular motion.

Forte watched from the walkway above the inside playground. Jackie Shaw stood next to him, watching him look down at the man with his niece. They could hear everything that was said in the courtyard by way of hidden microphones.

"Almost seems human, doesn't he?" she said.

"Funny thing is, he is a likeable guy, if you can ignore the destruction that he has caused in people's lives," he said.

"Nice of you to let him come visit," she said. "What made you do it?"

He turned his head and looked down at her. Her eyes were bright and expectant. He wondered how much she really knew about life. "Goodness of my heart?"

She shook her head slowly. "Ummm, don't think so."

"You don't really want to know," he said.

"Probably not. But it's a good thing. She was lonely for her family."

"Hopefully, it will all be over soon."

# Chapter 19

*Sunday, 5 p.m.*

The guitar was slightly out of tune but the boy playing it did a good job with the song anyway. His voice had a pure, clean sound that fit with the song, which talked of "a love that is fiercer than the love between friends, more gentle than a mother's with a baby at her side."

The singer stood at the front of a room with about fifty metal folding chairs arranged in rows and filled with people of every variety: street people with their ubiquitous plastic grocery bags and five-gallon plastic buckets with handles, strippers with teased hair and street clothes barely less garish than their on-the-job peel-away outfits, X-generation types in bowling shirts and baggy jeans. A few people were dressed more upscale. But not many.

Forte stood on the sidewalk barely outside the room leaning on the door jamb as he smoked Checkers number three and listened to the boy sing.

Just as the singer was wrapping it up, a man on the second row of chairs lurched forward and vomited. The people immediately surrounding him jumped out of the splash of his retching. Forte saw Manny jump up from the front row on the other side of the room and rush to a small closet off the meeting room. He came out with a rolling bucket and a mop and a roll of paper towels. He quickly mopped up the mess and wiped the man's face. Another man sitting behind him leaned forward, slapped the man on the back and chuckled.

Manny then stood up in front of the room, raised his hands and said, "May the Lord keep you in this coming week from relying on your own strength so that you may enjoy His love and peace more fully." The crowd of people milled around chatting and hugging each other. Manny stepped over to the man who had thrown up and put an arm around him. The man looked like he had drunk himself to sleep in a dumpster. Manny smiled and pulled out some money and put in the man's ragged coat pocket. He saw Forte and held up a finger that meant "wait a second."

Forte waited, feeling the nicotine do its work on him in the dwindling minutes of spring sunshine. The cigarette rush wasn't much but on a day like today, it was something to be thankful for. After the business with Poochie, he had left a message for Pastor Hamilton in Houston, asking if he knew anyone with police experience and to call him on his cell phone. He had made a few more phone calls, including one to his reporter pal Jonathan Brach who told him the FBI had a witness in the Lamberths' neighborhood who had seen a van parked on a side street near the Lamberth house around midnight. The authorities were asking the media not to release that information, Brach said, but he thought it might be helpful to Forte. No more word had come in from the kidnapper by phone or e-mail and the FBI didn't really expect any until the next day.

Nothing was happening with the Lamberth kidnapping but he had people checking on possibilities and he had a bit of information about the killer. Not much to work with but it was better than staring at a whiskey bottle and expecting an answer from it.

The meeting room for Manny's street church had finally cleared out. Manny walked over to him. "Still don't want to come in, huh?"

Forte pinched off the lit end of his cigarette and put it in his pocket. "Not today," he said.

"It's okay," Manny said. "You are here."

"You asked me to come see you," Forte said.

"Yes," said Manny. "Let's go upstairs."

Forte followed him up some stairs that led to a large apartment above the meeting room. The furniture was sturdy and the walls bare except for a single painting of an abstract woman dancing across slashes of red and yellow. A large honey-colored short-haired dog lay in front of the sofa. He looked up at Forte and huffed once then laid his head back on his paws. Forte sat on the couch and leaned forward to scratch the dog's ears. "Hey there, J.D.," he said to the animal.

The sounds of water running and dishes clinking came from the kitchen. Manny called out. "Tea?"

"Sure," Forte said.

A few more clinks and clanks came from the kitchen as Manny put the tea kettle on to boil. He came to the door of the den and stood with his arms crossed while he leaned on the wall. "Be just a sec," he said. "I saw it on the news, the Lamberth girl's kidnapping. Sounded hairy."

Forte stopped rubbing J.D.'s head and the dog nudged his hand. "Yeah," he said, "hairy."

"I'm sure there's more to it than the news said," Manny said.

Forte leaned back on the sofa cushions. J.D. huffed twice and raised his head to look at him, then lay back down. A pigeon landed on the ledge outside the screened open window and began its cooing as it paced back and forth with its head bobbing.

The tea kettle started whistling. Manny went to the kitchen and came back with two steaming mugs. He set one in front of Forte and sat in a faded blue easy chair.

"So," Manny said, "talk to me."

Forte sipped the orange flavored tea and talked. He told about the murder of the doctor, the call from Mrs. Lamberth, the situation with Poochie, the distraction of Freida, the kidnapping of the girl, the meeting with Jason Hamilton, and the dealings with Benny the counterfeiter. He realized as he talked that  the tension in his shoulders, that he hadn't even recognized, was easing .

Manny sat and listened, his blue eyes bright under bushy white brows as he looked at Forte over his mug of tea. He said nothing except an occasional "Yes" or "Hmmm" to keep the narrative moving along. At the end of it he said nothing.

Forte waited for a response. "Nothing to say about all this?" he said.

Manny sipped slowly. "Do I look like a psychologist?"

"You wanted me to tell you about everything."

"Yes. I didn't say I would tell you anything though."

"Oh I see. I blab and you say 'Hmmm'."

"About sums it up," Manny said. He sipped noiselessly. "Though I will say something if you want me to."

"Okay, say something," said Forte.

"What do you want me to say?"

Forte stared at him. "Is this a game or something?"

"No. I mean, if you were me, what would you say? What questions would you ask? Seriously."

Forte closed his eyes and rubbed his temples with the first two fingers on each hand. "I don't know. I'd ask ... if you thought you had completely failed. Could you have done anything different ... what bums you out most about all this ... what are you going to do next... questions along that line."

Manny nodded and set his mug on the table next to his chair. "And suppose I did ask you those questions, what would you say?"

Forte looked at the older man and thought for a moment. "I'd say 'Yes, I think I failed' and 'Maybe I should've not gone into Freida Lamberth's room' and 'The Lamberth girl being in danger and afraid makes me so damn mad when I think about it' and ..." He looked down at J.D. the dog then back at Manny. "What am I going to do next? I'm going to follow up on my leads from Benny."

Manny had closed his eyes and put his head back against the chair. "Sounds just about human to me."

Forte looked at him hard, then chuckled.

Manny smiled. "I am not making light of all this. It is serious stuff. It's just that sometimes we think everybody else has the answers and it turns out that our own answers, our own responses, turn out to be as good as anyone else could have come up with in the same set of circumstances." He opened his eyes. "And you didn't use cocaine over it. A good thing."

"Yeah."

Another pigeon landed on the window ledge. The two birds paced back and forth, their cooing mingled together like an atonal Oriental song.

"It's funny," Forte said. "The church thing, Hamilton's church. It got to me some."

"Oh?" Manny said.

"Yeah. It's like they were playing their weekly role for a couple of hours. Put on nice clothes. Act holy. Feel better about yourselves. Then go home and yell at your kids or cheat on your taxes." He looked at the birds on the ledge. "Not like your church downstairs anyway. I can see why you quit that big church in St. Louis."

Manny frowned. "I didn't quit. They fired me. For being a drunk. And a hypocrite. And you know what? They were right."

Forte grunted. "Well, you are better off now."

"I agree. But not because I got away from those church-role-playing people. I'm better off because I got broken."

Forte said nothing.

"And I bet there were some broken people there at the big church in Houston, too," Manny said. "But if I go around pointing out their brokenness before God has pointed it out to them, I will lose something and it won't just be their good favor. I will lose the understanding of what it really means to give love and to receive it." He paused and looked out the window, past the pigeons, at a point in the sky that no one else could see. "There are fools everywhere and we are included in that group. God bless us all." He focused on Forte again. "You may not see it now, but your own pain and brokenness have changed you. For the better."

Forte searched the older man's face for a moment. "Step by step," he said.

"Amen," said Manny.

# Chapter 20

*Sunday, 7 p.m.*

The killer clicked the mouse and scrolled down the list of hits that had come up in the search for "Al Forte." A dozen or so articles from the <u>Times-Picayune</u> web page, a feature story in <u>BODYGUARD</u> magazine, and several links to the Forte Security web page.

The day had been a long one. But the kidnapping of Hallee had gone exactly as planned. No one had been hurt. No bullet holes had marred the façade of the Lamberth mansion. He had put Hallee safely in the van and had driven across the bridge to the house in Gretna, pulling into the garage around back under the cover of night. No one had taken notice. The girl had not awakened until she was safely locked in her room.

She had awakened screaming. He had spoken to her calmly through the door, explaining to her that she would not be harmed as long as her mother came through with the ransom money. Eventually Hallee had stopped pounding on the walls and yelling. He had spent several days fortifying the room with soundproofing, especially over the window. The room had clothes, a bed and a chair, a television, and a refrigerator stocked with food. She would be as comfortable as she chose to be. Besides, she would only be there for a day and a night if everything worked out as planned.

He had already written the specific directions for the ransom. The e-mail message rested digitally on the laptop's hard drive, in the Drafts folder of his Outlook Express program. The e-mail message – which eventually would be forwarded through several blind e-mail boxes – would be sent before noon the next day, Monday. It read:

```
Make preparations to phone the Nassau
International Bank at exactly 4:30 p.m.
today (Monday). Wire the money to account
#Z498B-211Q5530. The bank will be expecting
your call.
     No excuses will be accepted for your
failure to send the $25 million. Your
failure will result in the disappearance
forever of Hallee Lamberth.
     It is not my desire to harm the child,
believe me. When I verify that the money
has been transferred, I will contact you
with directions immediately on where to
pick up your daughter, healthy and
unharmed.
```

Now, however, he was trying to appease a curiosity that had been growing stronger and stronger during the past couple of days. Who was Al Forte? He had known of the man before but there was something about him that bore closer scrutiny. The man seemed relentless, not easily derailed from what he thought he should do. A trait to be admired for sure, the killer thought, but one that could cause trouble for the operation.

During the previous night, when he had taken Hallee, the killer had made it all the way back to the van before Forte had discovered the girl was missing. He  had watched on the monitors as Forte had immediately leaped through the window and onto the roof, scrambling in pursuit. There had been no hesitation. The killer mentally congratulated himself for the detailed planning he had done.

Forte's lightening response could have endangered a more casually-run operation.

Perhaps the man needed another distraction or two to take his attention off the Lamberth case. He picked up his cell phone, called a number, spoke a few words into the phone and hung up. He turned back to the computer.

The killer clicked and scrolled through screen after screen of information about Forte. After an hour or so of reading, he had begun to piece together the background of Al Forte.

Forte was born February 29, 1964 on a Saturday at Keesler Air Force Base Hospital in Biloxi, Mississippi. His dad was not a flyer, however, but was in the Navy Seabees, which had an installation there at the base. Both of his parents were killed in a car accident in the summer of 1971. He went to live with his grandmother, who managed a liquor store in New Orleans. The grandmother died in her sleep six years later and Forte was virtually homeless at age 13.

The information was sketchy about his teen years but it seemed that a friend of the grandmother's, an old Creole barber, had taken the boy into his home.

The killer stopped scrolling the computer screen, closed his eyes and tried to imagine what that must have been like. He had few points of reference himself, having grown up in an orphanage. He opened his eyes and kept reading.

There were sports stories on Forte's days as a high school football player. He had played for St. Joseph High School in the parochial league and had been quite effective at the linebacker position. One article referred to him as "Alvin the Anvil" because opposing running backs were "stopped cold" when they ran into him. A few scholarship offers had come his way, but he opted to join the Navy after graduation.

He excelled in the armed services and after a year or so made it into the elite training program for Navy SEALs. The Sea/Air/Land commandos were under the direction of the Naval Special Warfare division and were reputed to be the toughest of the U.S. military's special forces. Forte had distinguished himself early as a SEAL in Panama as part of Operation Just Cause and again in Desert Strike a couple of years later.

During a furlough trip back to New Orleans, Forte had met a social worker named Ruth Blaise. Within the year, the two married but the relationship was fairly short-lived. The wife was murdered in 1994 by a teenage gang member in a midtown alley. Apparently the eighth-grade boy had been a client of the woman's and the death was the result of a gang initiation prank gone wrong. Unbeknownst to the boy, someone had loaded bullets in the gun, which was supposed to have been empty.

Forte had tracked down the boy and had, by his own admission, been an inch away from murdering the teenager in an act of cold-blooded vengeance. His own anger terrified him. He caught himself in time, but he was crushed by the loss. For a period of nearly two years following his wife's death, he came apart at the seams. He tried unsuccessfully to make the pain go away with liquor and after one particular month-long drinking binge, he graduated to cocaine. He drifted through a haze of booze and white powder for months before waking up in a detox unit at Tulane Medical Center. A friend of his, Manning Laird, had found him close to death in his apartment and had rushed him to the hospital.

After a six-month stint in a drug treatment center in Florida, Forte had resolved to use his talents for a good purpose. He had used inheritance money to start The Refuge, a shelter for children in extreme danger. After a year he had turned over the shelter's day-to-day operations to an independent board and had opened his own company, Forte Security, specializing in the protection and recovery of kidnapped children.

The first major assignment for his new business had been to find and bring back a local boy who had been stolen by a disgruntled New Orleans city employee. The boy was the grandson of long-time city councilman Thomas Christenberry, a man of no small financial and political means. The New Orleans police and FBI had spent a week making no headway on the case. Forte had found the boy in Italy and had brought him home safely within three days. The kidnapper and an accomplice had been killed during the rescue. Old man Christenberry, who died of cancer within six months of the kidnap recovery, had set up and endowed a foundation in his will that reputedly would fund the operation of The Refuge amply for as long as Forte cared to keep it in existence.

Since that time, more high-profile cases had come his way, boosting Forte's reputation until he was recognized as one of the foremost experts in kidnap recovery in the world. He refused all cases, however, except for those involving children. He said he had decided on that particular refinement of his mission in honor of his late wife.

The killer leaned back in his chair, rubbed his eyes and got up. Television noises, muted by the soundproofing, came from Hallee's room. He stepped to the bedroom door and knocked. "Everything okay in there?" he asked. The girl did not answer but the volume decreased on the TV set. "Answer me now, Hallee," he said, louder.

Her voice came back more clearly than he expected. She was apparently standing on the other side of the door. "I'm here," she said.

"Do you need anything?"

"No. Except to go home."

"You will see your mom tomorrow."

There was no response now.

He stood at the door, listening. "Get some rest," he said. He walked back to the computer desk. He looked at the screen again then walked into the den and stood at the picture window overlooking the sleepy Gretna street in front of the house.

He imagined that happy families lived in all the quaint houses up and down this street and throughout this neighborhood. It had that kind of homey feel to it. Middle class folks with average kids and mediocre dreams of paying off the mortgage and someday collecting that pension so the grandkids could come for a week or two each summer. People not unhappy with the lot they had chosen. People with their heads in the sand. People without a mission in life and most of them unaware of the need for one.

He had a mission. And Forte had one. They were alike in that respect, he mused. They were both dedicated to their goals. In a way, he regretted that Forte had to be his enemy. If the man had seen the things he had seen, he probably would be on his side. But as his second foster-dad had often said, "You gotta play the cards you're dealt."

He turned away from the window and went back to the computer. He clicked on the Favorites icon and navigated through the World Wide Web to his favorite chat room: StrikeBack. It was devoted to the discussion of using lethal force to protect the unborn. He logged on as KillShine, one of his chat nicknames, and entered the room. Five people were there already and a discussion was in progress, as usual.

> **Swordsman:** Oh, I agree that the guy did a good job taking out the doctor. I just don't see why he had to kidnap the girl.
> **Angelfist:** I don't get that either.
> **BreakMan:** Maybe he wants to make a stronger statement. Like an eye for an eye. A child for a child.
> **Swordsman:** Or a child for a million children.
> **BreakMan:** Millions of children since Roe in '73.

No one typed anything for a few moments. In the house in Gretna, the monitor bathed the darkened room with an eerie light.

Another person joined the online conversation, someone who had been lurking in the chatroom, not saying anything. The killer had not seen him in the room before. His nickname was Rescuer.

> **Rescuer:** That's not right. An innocent child's life traded for another innocent child or a million more innocent children. It's just one more wrong.
> **Angelfist:** Yeah I agree with that.
> **BreakMan:** Maybe he wouldn't really kill her. Maybe he just wants the money.
> **Rescuer:** So then he's just a pure capitalist like everyone else. Like the abortion doctors themselves.

The man in the Gretna house frowned at the screen. What does this guy know. He let his fingers clatter over the keyboard and watched his comment come up on the screen.

> **KillShine:** Maybe there are other reasons. More complicated.
> **Rescuer:** REASONS Like what?
> **KillShine:** Like … he thinks the blood money that came from all those dead children can be used…. can be redeemed… to … further the cause.
> **Rescuer:** The cause. Right.

*Who is this guy?!!*

> **KillShine:** Yes, the cause of defending innocent children from murderers.
> **Rescuer:** So the life of this child can be sacrificed then, in the name of the cause.
> **KillShine:** She won't be …

The killer reached to hit the delete key but hit the Enter key from force of habit. He stared at his words on the screen. The person named Rescuer questioned the statement immediately.

> **Rescuer:** She won't be? SHE WON'T BE WHAT??

The killer slammed his hands on the table, making the keyboard jump. He logged off.

* * *

At his office, Forte sat and stared at his computer screen. What had happened?

Who was KillShine?

He drummed his fingers on the desk and waited for him to log back into the chat room. Finally he leaned forward and typed two words. His words appeared on the screen:

**Rescuer:** Logging off.

He reached over and clicked off his desk light.

# Chapter 21

Jackie Shaw maneuvered the van through the narrow streets of the Quarter, being careful to keep her turns slow so the grocery bags behind her seat wouldn't tip over. On the radio, a Janet Jackson tune blared out. Something about nasty boys. Jackie was paying little attention. Nasty boys? *Popular music has become so enlightening these days.*

She was being careful to watch for anyone tailing her on her way back and forth from the shelter to the grocery store. Everything seemed normal for a Sunday evening in New Orleans. Some of the residents of the area strolling back from a walk in the park. A few joggers and cyclists grabbing some exercise before the next morning's return to the weekly grind. No bad guys in sight. A quiet night.

She had been secretly glad that the regular grocery delivery had been cancelled. She didn't even care to know why the grocer had dropped the ball. She was just glad to get out for a few minutes. As much as she loved her new job at the Refuge, she had gone too long without taking the free time that was due her. It was her fault. She had felt a special bond with the little girl Kyra. No one should have to deal with the murder of her own father by being locked away.

It made Jackie's throat constrict to think about what that must feel like.

The grocery trip had been therapeutic. Squeezing the tomatoes, shaking the melons, sniffing the flowers. She had stretched her shopping time out a little longer than planned but they could give her a break. The Refuge was locked up tighter than Dick's hat band with two burly guards on duty, a closet full of automatic weapons, and cameras everywhere. Dick's hat band? One of her Dad's favorite expressions.

Now, she was delivering the goods safely back home. She smiled to herself. Home. She already thought of if that way. Most people would hesitate to consider this unnatural setting a "home." But she was accustomed to unusual circumstances. Maybe that's why she was drawn to the job. She had not felt such a sense of purpose in anything she had done before.

Jackie slowed the van for the final turn onto the street that ran behind the shelter. As she approached the garage door she scanned both sides of the street. Nothing was moving. She reached for the remote to open the garage door.

Boom! Crash! The rear window of the van exploded.

Jackie ducked as the shower of Plexiglas pebbles ricocheted against the metal walls inside the van.

Boom! Another shotgun blast hit the back door of the van.

An alarm went off next to the garage door. Everything seemed to slow down and come into sharp focus now for Jackie.

She jammed her hand into her purse and brought out a compact nine-millimeter automatic. She quickly checked the rearview mirror for anyone approaching her side of the van. Nothing.

She rammed the door with her shoulder at the same instant she pulled the door latch and rolled out on the pavement next to the van. Across the street in a doorway stood a man with a shotgun. Jackie leveled her gun at him and squeezed off two rapid shots.

The man scrambled backward out of sight.

Lying flat on her stomach, Jackie spun to her left. She looked under the van, between the tires for movement. She could only see a man's legs and they were edging toward the van.

Cha-chunk. The sound of another shell being shucked into the chamber. Boom! The person on the other side of the van blasted away at the vehicle.

Jackie carefully put the sights of her gun on the approaching man's right foot. Crack! Her handgun bucked slightly in her hand but the bullet found the attacker's foot. The man screamed and fell to the pavement. His shotgun clattered away from him on the street. Jackie could see the man's face, a mask of pain, as he writhed on the street surface just a few feet away from her.

Thank you, Dad, for making me take all that target practice, Jackie thought. She knew help would show up soon. Only seconds had passed. She must keep the other gunman away.

Boom! Jackie felt something sting her leg. The attacker across the street had opened fire again. She scrambled under the van on her stomach. Boom! Another blast hit the van. Blam! The front tire closest to her blew out.

She peeked from behind the back tire of the van and leveled her gun at the man with the shotgun. Crack! Crack! Crack! She sent three rounds at the doorway across the street. The barrel of the shotgun pulled back quickly.

The alarm on the wall next to the garage door was deafening now.

Her leg was stinging. She put her hand on her thigh and felt a spot of wet the size of her palm. It didn't feel serious. Yet.

Boom! Boom! She cringed. These shotgun blasts came from her left. But they didn't hit the van. They were directed at the man across the street.

She felt a twinge in her leg as she scooted forward for a better look at the action. The man across the street stuck his barrel out and fired without looking where his blast went. Three quick blasts came back at him. He poked his head out quickly and looked toward the left of the opposite corner diagonally. The attacker dashed for the corner on his side of the street. Boom! A blast followed him. He took another wild shot from the corner.

A long black car shot through the intersection at the corner and screeched to a halt. From her vantage point, Jackie could see the man turn to look at the car. He looked confused. Two large men jumped out of the car and grabbed the gunman, who struggled but did not try to shoot them. They threw him into the back seat of the car. It screeched away.

Jackie laid her head on her arm, which was stretched in front of her under the van. To her left, she heard the sound of footsteps.

Then Forte yelling "Stay down or you are dead!" The injured gunman Jackie had shot lay on the ground clutching his foot, moaning and muttering in Spanish. He made no sudden moves.

More footsteps approached on the run. Someone shouted, "Any more of them?" She recognized the voice of one of the shelter's security guards.

"Looks like all of them," Forte shouted back. "Jackie?"

She suddenly felt very tired. And dirty. Street grime covered the front of her shirt and jeans. The van's radio sounded other-worldly from underneath the vehicle. "Under here," she said.

Hands reached and pulled her out as gently as possible. She was placed on the sidewalk. On her thigh she could see a large dark blotch of scarlet. "Sit back," Forte said. His hands probed along her leg. She winced. He took out a knife and cut away the denim around the blood-soaked spot. He dabbed at the wound and she jerked again. "Sorry," he said. "The wound is going to annoy you but it's not bad. A stray pellet got you."

She nodded. Her eyes had been squeezed together. She opened them and saw the look on Forte's face. She was startled. A chill ran down the back of her neck. His face looked calm but his eyes ... those yellow eyes. Behind them boiled a storm of anger, controlled for the moment but needing release. Soon.

Jackie closed her eyes again. An ambulance siren sounded somewhere in the distance. She turned to ask Forte if she really needed to go to the hospital. She opened her eyes.

He was gone.

# Chapter 22

*Sunday, 10:30 p.m.*

Forte walked along the opposite side of the street staying in the shadows of the oak trees as he circled the mansion for the second time. It took a while to completely circumnavigate the estate. The house was twice as big as the Lamberth house. The wall was higher and thicker and topped with razor wire. The mansion occupied an entire block.

A palace fit for a Colombian drug lord.

As he had sped through the black streets of Metairie on the way to the house, his rage had mounted. The attacks must stop. He had imagined blasting through the gate and riding his motorcycle up the stairs to pin Ricardo Aguilar to the wall. That fantasy balloon had burst quickly when he saw the house. Now that he had calmed down, he knew that a platoon of Marines would incur many casualties getting into Aguilar's home. He had to assume that several guards armed with submachine guns patrolled the grounds and that more guards would be on duty inside the house. The drug lord was also sure to have plenty of high-scale surveillance equipment everywhere on the property too.

Forte completed his circle of the block and sat side-saddle on his motorcycle. He took out a cigarette and lit it. No better time than the present to smoke Checkers number five. He looked along the long expanse of thick brick wall as he smoked. He had no doubt that, even now, his image was being picked up by some hidden video camera and displayed on a monitor inside the house.

The front gate of the mansion abruptly whirred and swung open. A long black Lincoln Town Car eased out of the driveway onto the street.

Forte held his cigarette in his mouth and leaned down to retrieve his shotgun from the holster mounted on his bike. The car slowly turned in his direction and crept toward him. Forte shucked a shell into the firing chamber and thumbed off the safety. By the time the car was level with him he had the gun leveled at the side windows.

The car idled for a moment. Forte could see nothing but his own distorted reflection with the cigarette dangling from his mouth in the dark tinted windows. He waited.

After a moment the back rear window closest to him slid down a couple of inches.

"Buenos noches, Senor," a man's voice said. The man's face was still out of sight.

Forte nodded and kept the gun steady.

"Can we help you with something?" The man's tone was polite but insistent.

"Yes," Forte said. "You can tell your boss to stop his attacks or I will bring some of my friends over and we will make life very unpleasant for him."

A laugh came from someone inside the car but the man who had first spoken to Forte did not respond for a moment. A flurry of Spanish flew around the inside of the car. The window lowered a few more inches. "That is your message, senor?" The man's voice sounded amused now.

"Si," said Forte.

The window closed and the car backed up. It turned up the driveway. The gate shut behind it.

Forte flicked his ashes and waited. He had finished the cigarette by the time the gate opened again.

The car pulled up to him and the window opened again. "If you please," the same voice said in precise English, "Senor Aguilar invites you to his home to speak with him."

"Now?" Forte said.

"Si."

Forte swung his legs over his bike. "I'll follow you," he said. He kicked the starter pedal and the motorcycle started up.

"As you wish, senor." The black car pulled away and Forte followed.

The driveway ended at a six-car garage behind the house. The car stopped next to a covered overhang at the end of the house. Four men got out of the car and walked toward him. All were oversized and each had bulges under their coats exactly where a shoulder holster would be.

The spokesman of the group was tall with black hair pulled into a ponytail. His face showed no emotion as he spoke. "You must leave your weapons here, please," he said.

"No," Forte said.

The man shrugged. "It is the rules. You will be safe. Your guns will be returned to you when you leave."

Forte looked at the four men. No smiles. No hard looks. Just business. He let his gaze sweep across the house. He quickly counted a half-dozen other guards on balconies and patios. His weapons would do him little good anyway.

He took out the nine millimeter automatic at the small of his back. He bent down and pulled out the .380 automatic in his boot. He took both of his throwing knives from their hidden sheaths where they were tucked on each side of the waistband of his pants. He handed them over. One of the four men stepped over and pulled his shotgun from its holster on the bike.

Forte followed the spokesman into the house. A fountain sparkled in the center of a tiled foyer that was bigger than the entire first floor of his apartment. The entry room emptied into an even larger dining room with three large openings. On the right was a sitting room, on the left was a corridor leading to the kitchen, and straight ahead Forte could see a sweeping stairway leading up to a circular landing. He followed his guide up the stairs. At a heavy oak door, they stopped. The other man opened the door and held out his hand for Forte to walk ahead into the room.

On a large table in the middle of the room stood a half-finished wood carving of a horse. The front half of the horse was rearing in the air, mane flying and eyes wild. The rear half of the horse did not yet exist, remaining encased in the sun-bleached driftwood log on the table. A wooden case with various carving tools lay open next to the carving.

A powerful-looking man was bent over the wood, carefully digging out curls of white wood with a slender instrument. His sleeves were rolled up. His salt-and-pepper hair was slicked back on his tanned head. For another full minute the only sound in the room was the snick-snick of the man at work. It looked incongruous to Forte, the man's thick fingers as they maneuvered the small tool to bring out the beauty of the carving. But then again, it seemed to work for him.

Finally he stopped and stepped back. He walked around the carving once then took a towel out of his belt and slapped it against the horse several times to knock the sawdust away. Only then did he look over at Forte. He smiled broadly and extended his hand.

"Good evening, Mr. Forte. Welcome to the humble home of Ricardo Aguilar."

Forte looked at the man's hand and shook it. He could feel the calluses in the man's strong grip.

Aguilar folded the wiping towel neatly and placed it on the corner of the table. He motioned to the man who had led Forte up the stairs and the man went to a teak cabinet, opened it and brought out a polished wooden box about a foot square. Aguilar took a seat in an oxblood leather chair and waved a hand at the matching leather divan for Forte to sit. He did.

The assistant brought the box to Aguilar and held it open. The drug lord. selected a cigar and began rolling it between his fingertips. "Thank you, Manolo," he said. The man brought the cigar box to Forte. He held up his hand to signal no.

From the table next to his chair Aguilar picked up a bone-handled folding knife, flipped open the blade, and, with precise movements, cut the tip off the cigar.

Forte sat and watched the man, knowing that the drug boss had reached the point where he could live his life with such nonchalant ease. The slashing and screaming and undiluted hands-on violence had come earlier in his career. Not that those times were over forever.

Manolo stepped forward again and lit Aguilar's cigar with a silver lighter. The drug lord closed his eyes and drew in the smoke, held it, then released it. "Ahhh," he said as he exhaled. "Magnifico."

He opened his eyes and watched the smoke drift to the ceiling. "Mr. Forte," he said without looking at him, "have you ever seen an albino horse?"

Forte looked at the man. "No."

Aguilar puffed again and put his head back. "The albino is a freak; it is born with no pigment in its skin or eyes. A beautiful animal. So innocent, so pure. And valuable. Would you like to know why?" He puffed again and continued without waiting for a response. "Because when it is bred, the albino passes along none of its own traits. The resulting foal is the exact replica in coloring to the other horse that mates with the albino. It is guaranteed. For as long as it lives, the albino horse fulfils its role in life exactly the way it should, every time."

He looked at Forte now. "I admire that," he said, "because predictability is a rare thing in the world we live in, wouldn't you agree?" He puffed again, his eyes closed. He turned to Forte. "Thank you for indulging my idle rambling, my friend. To what do we owe this visit?"

"Stop coming after the girl," Forte said.

Aguilar arched his heavy eyebrows slightly. "The girl. Kyra, the daughter of the man who was killed." It was a statement, not a question. "Tell me, Senor Forte. If I were interested in capturing this girl, what makes you think you could stop me?"

Forte could not tell if the glint in the other man's eye was amusement or annoyance.

"My resourcefulness and dogged determination?"

Aguilar threw his head back and laughed, his cigar waving over the Persian rug. "Manolito, here is a man who enjoys life on the edge. We could learn much from him, eh?"

Forte leaned forward, his hands on his knees. "Mr. Aguilar, I am your guest here tonight. I must be direct with you, however. If there is another attack on the shelter, I will bring back more people the next time I come here. We will do whatever it takes to stop you. Guaranteed. I am kind of predictable like that."

Aguilar rolled the cigar in his hands. "You do enjoy the edge of the cliff, senor." His eyes had lost their humor. He held Forte's stare for what seemed like a full minute. Then he regained a hard smile. "But I admire your courage. Come, my friend. Let me show you something."

Manolo was on his feet, opening the door. Forte followed Aguilar out of the room, down the stairs and across the back lawn. A smaller building that matched the house in design and color was on the back corner of the property surrounded by trees. A man-made goldfish pond bordered the manicured walkway leading to the building. There was a large drive-through door on one side of the building and a regular door next to it. A man was guarding the door, an automatic rifle at ready position. He stepped aside and swung open the door as his boss approached.

Inside on the concrete floor were three large riding mowers, four push mowers, two small garden tractors. Weed trimmers, leaf blowers, shovels, hoes, and rakes hung from organizer racks along one wall. The opposite wall was covered with shelves laden with various weed poisons and fertilizers.

In the far corner, behind one of the riding mowers, sat the man who had shot up the van at the Refuge.

He was shirtless and his belt was unbuckled. A crimson trickle came from the corner of his mouth. A yellow bandana was tied tight between his lips. His left eye was swollen shut. His hands were tied behind the wooden chair. His right eye shone with terror as Aguilar approached him. The man flinched when the drug lord laid a hand gently on his shoulder.

In the harsh light of the bare overhead bulb in the storage building, Aguilar's face was all hard angles. "This is Jorge, the man who shot at you, no? Unfortunately, Jorge has not proven to be a very predictable and dependable member of our family. He has engaged in some… how do you say it… extracurricular activities."

Jorge's right eye rolled in fear.

The drug lord untied the bandana in the man's mouth.

"Jorge," he said softly, "tell this man who hired you to attack his organization."

Jorge tried to speak. His voice croaked but no words would come. Aguilar motioned to Manolo who stepped over to a refrigerator by the door. He brought out a bottle of water, uncapped it, and held it to the bound man's lips. Water ran out of the corners of his mouth and dribbled down his chest. The man gulped noisily then gagged and erupted in a fit of coughing. He bent over as far as the duct tape that held him to the chair would allow, then straightened again.

Aguilar spoke again, his voice louder now. "Tell him, Jorge."

The man in the chair looked at Forte with his one good eye. "A man," he croaked. "Long hair. Black hair." He tried to say more but nothing came out. His voice sounded as if he had screamed himself hoarse. The right eye moved back to focus on the drug lord.

Forte pulled out the ID photos he had been given by Benny the counterfeiter. He found the one of the clinic employee Brent Garrison and held it up in front of the man's face. The bound man pulled his head back and looked at the picture. He nodded.

Forte turned to Aguilar. "Thank you."

The drug lord turned and walked out of the building. Forte and Manolo followed him.

Aguilar stopped by the goldfish pond and turned to face Forte. The lights that illuminated the pool gave the drug lord's face a deceptive softness. "Things are not always as they appear, eh, Mr. Forte?" He watched a foot-long goldfish dart up from the depths of the pool, then disappear into the water beneath the lily pads. "This business I am in, it is a hard business at times. I know this and am not shy about doing the hard things that are sometimes required. I am not, however, without compassion. I know about the girl who was kidnapped." He stooped and picked up a small jar on the stone border of the fish pond. He twisted the top off the jar, scooped out some of the fish food flakes, and sprinkled them over the pond. Immediately several fish thrashed to the surface of the water in competition for the food. Aguilar set the jar on the stones again and stood up.

"Jorge will make a statement to the police about the attacks on your shelter. He will not give the police the location of the man who hired him. Because he does not know his location." He snapped his finger and Manolo stepped forward with a small piece of paper. He handed it to Forte. On it were written two things: an address in Gretna and a description of a vehicle.

"I took the liberty of having Jorge followed once my operation was accused of the attacks on you. Obviously, I knew that the orders to attack you did not come from me. I wanted to know who gave them. Manolo here had the good sense to follow the man who hired Jorge. He trailed the man back to the address on that piece of paper. Now you know what we know. We are out of it.

"I apologize for Jorge's behavior. Since he is part of my family here, I must take responsibility for him. I hope this bit of information will balance the scales between us, you and me, Senor Forte."

Forte tucked the paper into his pocket. "Thank you," he said.

Aguilar nodded. "Vaya con Dios," he said.

# Chapter 23

The bar at The Beauxgard was half-full, which was not bad for a Sunday night, even in New Orleans. Especially since it was not located in the French Quarter. Then again, this was no regular bar.

The Beauxgard had been one of the plantation houses along St. Charles built in the early 17th century. Acres and acres of sugar cane had stretched out behind and beside the house with its sturdy white columns and broad front porch. Like many of the regal homesteads in and around the city, it had survived both the War of 1812 and the Union capture of New Orleans during the Civil War.

Now it was a stately hotel for those travelers who wanted more of a taste of the old South than the all-night party atmosphere that pervaded the French Quarter. The Beauxgard's décor had been restored to its original luster and, better yet, it had been replumbed and rewired to please the most modern tourist's taste for convenience.

The bar was the old mansion's crowning achievement, according to the travel guides. Rich dark mahogany covered the walls and ceiling. A cozy bar with gleaming brass rails and footrests was backgrounded by a mural of a plantation scene along the river. A

19th-century country gentleman stepping into the room after a long day's journey on horseback would have been satisfied.

When Forte walked in, couples and trios of people had spread out among the tables in the candle-lit lounge area. A couple of men sat at the bar with three stools between them as they tipped glasses of amber liquid to their mouths. A woman played a Cole Porter song on the baby grand piano in the far corner of the room.

Forte sat at the end of the bar away from the door. He sat with his back against the bar, listening to the music. He had seen this scene a hundred times before but with different eyes. At this point in his life, the place seemed comfortable, a quiet stop for a bit of relaxed conversation. During his years of grief it would have been a place of escape for him, a haven from reality. Behind him, he heard the chop-chopping of the bartender at his cutting board.

The piano player's song ended. Forte turned and watched the man behind the bar as he sliced lemons and scooped the slices into a clear glass container with a snap-on lid. The bartender's movements were quick and practiced. Each lemon slice looked exactly the same as the slice before it, from where Forte sat.

"Water, with a twist," Forte said.

One of the men at the other end of the bar looked over at him then quickly looked back at his drink. The bartender glanced up. He set his knife on the edge of the cutting board and wiped his hands on his apron.

Forte had left Aguilar's place and had driven straight to his office. He had located the address that the drug lord had given him on a detailed street map of Gretna. Then he had packed up the equipment he needed in a large duffel bag and loaded it into his black van. He had driven straight to The Beauxgard.

The bartender brought his drink. As he placed it on the napkin in front of Forte, he could see the tattoo of a seal on the inside of the man's forearm. A woman came in and sat two stools down from

Forte. The bartender took her order, filled it, then came back to where Forte sat.

"Thanks, Nomad," Forte said.

"Long time," said the bartender.

"Three months since the last time," Forte said.

Mike "Nomad" Jones worked the bar at The Beauxgard but few people knew he actually owned the hotel. And that was exactly how he wanted it. He worked the bar a few nights a week because he enjoyed it and because the steady stream of movers and shakers through the bar kept him abreast of what was really going on in the city. He once told Forte that his whole life was undercover. The things Nomad did when he was away from the hotel for a week or two, Forte didn't ask and his friend didn't tell.

The two had trained and worked together as Navy SEALS. The man looked the least like a special forces commando of anyone in the unit. His nationality defied guessing but Nomad liked calling himself a "mongrel of American Indian, African, Irish and Saudi extraction." Though one of the smallest of the training group, Jones had earned a reputation for toughness early on. Whenever an exercise was given to the trainees by the drillmasters, someone in the group would point out a possible obstacle. Jones's answer was always the same: No matter. Except it came out "Nomadda" in Jones's low voice. When it came to pure guts, no one matched him.

Forte had seen him in action in Panama and in Iraq. He had heard of Nomad's exploits rescuing two of his wounded squad members during the fiasco in Somalia. That major screwup by the military higher-ups had prompted Nomad to go out on his own. He had moved to New Orleans and bought the hotel. Forte never asked exactly where he got the money for the purchase.

The piano player began another set of standards, starting with "Blue Moon." One of the men at the other end of the bar had moved down with his drink to sit next to the woman. Forte could hear nothing but whispers and ice clinking.

"You get off soon?" Forte asked Nomad.

"Whenever I want," Nomad said, polishing a glass and looking out over the room.

"Got a mission. Quick and dirty. No time for planning," Forte said.

Nomad smiled. "Right down my alley." He set the glass on the bar. "Something to do with the Lamberth thing?"

Forte put a finger to his lips. "Shhhh." He leaned forward. "This has everything to do with it."

Nomad nodded. "I'm in."

Forte took a folded sheet of paper out of his pocket. He slid it across the bar. "Here's the equipment list you'll need. I'll be waiting in my van out back."

Nomad unfolded the paper and scanned the list. He smiled more broadly now. "Gretna?" He looked up at Forte. "Let's rock and roll."

Forte took a last sip of his drink and made a face.

Nomad took the glass away. "The price of purity, huh?"

Forte stood up. "The price of sanity."

\* \* \*

After Forte left, the woman at the bar waited a few minutes then quickly excused herself from the cloying company of the man trying to pick her up. She walked to the ornate restroom and peeked under each stall to make sure she was alone.

She opened her purse and took out a cell phone. She dialed a number and spoke in quiet but urgent tones, then hung up.

She had been surprised to get a call from the blond man who had hired her to have dinner with him at Mack's. No sex, just dinner. It had been a chore to act relaxed and to laugh at the man's stories. Something about him seemed chilling. But this little assignment had been easy.

She dropped the phone back into her purse and snapped it shut. After a minute or so in front of the mirror to adjust her wig, she walked out of the bar.

# Chapter 24

*Monday, 1:45 a.m.*

The house was dark except for two rooms. A faint flickering came from the den, probably from a television set. In one of the bedrooms, the greenish light of a computer monitor shone on the walls and ceiling.

Forte squatted behind a stand of azaleas in the back yard of the house in Gretna. "Any movement?" he whispered into his headset microphone.

"Nothing so far," responded Nomad from his position in the bushes along the front of the house.

Both men were outfitted in night-camouflage with Kevlar vests and Kevlar leg protectors. They both carried short-barreled shotguns fitted with pistol grips and seven-round magazines. The first two rounds in each gun were non-lethal, a condition Forte insisted on and to which Nomad reluctantly agreed. The last five shells in each magazine meant business. Each man had two flash-bang grenades hanging from his belt. Nine millimeter handguns were snug in shoulder holsters with the safeties off.

They were as ready as they could be, given the urgency of their mission.

They had driven past the house a half-hour earlier, circled the block and passed it again. Only one house in the neighborhood, several streets over, showed any signs of anyone being awake. The lights were completely doused in all five of the homes with back yards connecting to the kidnapper's house. Only one of the connecting houses – the one directly behind – looked empty. The carport of that house was vacant. Two newspapers lay at the end of the driveway.

Forte had slowed the van in front of the house and Nomad had leaped from the vehicle and scurried up to the carport. He rang the doorbell and listened for any sound inside. He rang again. When you have no time to plan, he mused, the simplest tactic is the best. No one stirred inside the house. "It's clear," he said into his microphone. Forte circled back with the van and pulled into the carport. They stopped and watched the surrounding houses for any signs that the neighbors had stirred. Everything stayed dark and quiet except for a dog barking somewhere in the distance.

Ordinarily it would have taken sixty seconds or less to jog over to the common fence that formed the back yard divider for the two houses, vault it, and trot around the house to check for any movement. Ordinarily. Forte and Nomad filled half an hour with their initial reconnaissance of the kidnapper's hideout as they moved a few feet, stopped and watched for any indication they had drawn attention. The approach to the house had to be executed perfectly. Any sound could alert the neighborhood. At best, a neighbor would mistake them for burglars and call the police. At worst, the kidnapper would spy them and open fire.

The house was quiet. Curtains were drawn in the room on the corner of the house that faced the back yard. Forte guessed the curtained room was a bedroom, and that Hallee was in it. The blinds were open on the other windows around the house. A careless mistake by the kidnapper, Forte thought, to allow visual entry to the house. Nomad had climbed a tree in the neighbor's yard and, looking through a night-vision scope into the other bedroom, had seen a figure sitting at the desk with the computer. A sniper shot could take him out.

But they had to play by a certain set of rules on this night, unlike some of their covert missions as SEALs in the past. Those missions had been the kind not reported in any of the official accounts of the Navy's engagements. No one ever spoke of those off-the-book missions but they had been carried out. And carried out efficiently.

On this night they could not be absolutely sure where the girl was located inside the house. Even if they were inclined to assassinate the kidnapper with a sniper's bullet, they would still be taking a chance that the bullet would pass through the body of the kidnapper and hit Hallee also. After everything that had happened up to this point, that risk was unacceptable.

Forte sat with his back against a tree trunk behind the azalea bushes, watching the house for any shadows moving across the walls. He had watched the window long enough to memorize the types of patterns sprinkled on the ceiling by the television set. He let his head move from side to side very slowly every minute or so, relying on his peripheral vision to catch any out-of-place movement in the yards surrounding him. There was no moon tonight but swirls of stars covered the cloudless sky. A gentle breeze blew through the branches above where he sat. He could hear the leaves whispering in the wind. The smell of flowers he could not name flowed over him. A perfect night for a strike.

He had not realized how numb the kidnapping had left him. Never had someone in his protection been plucked from beneath his nose while he was on guard. He knew it was his pride that was suffering. Failure was the thing that terrified him more than anything else. He had failed, there was no denying that. Others could talk about the advantages the kidnapper had over him because of the camera surveillance and the rigged alarm system. He could not let himself off the hook so easily. No, there was only one way to redeem himself: get the girl back. He had lost her. He would recover her.

He rubbed a hand over his eyes. He felt more at ease now than he had been at any time since the kidnapping. He knew why. He was doing something he was trained to do. From his first mock mission as a SEAL, he had known that this work was what he was born to do. When his team members had been practically puking on their boots with nerves, he had been surprised by his calmness. After that he had grown to accept it.

He and Nomad had hashed out an attack strategy during the drive over the bridge to Gretna. First, determine if the kidnapper was still awake. Second, as much as was possible, identify which room the kidnapper was in and which room held Hallee. Third, create a diversion. The entry would be timed so that Nomad tossed a flash-bang grenade through the window at the same instant Forte blew open the back door with his shotgun. Fourth, subdue the kidnapper and recover Hallee. Forte would blast the stunned kidnapper with his non-lethal charges while Nomad found the girl. Fifth, get away as fast as possible. The neighborhood would be ablaze with lights after the flash bomb, but by then the mission would be over. Getting out safe was what mattered.

Not a great plan but it was all they had to work with. The element of surprise would give them an advantage. The kidnapper would be looking forward to collecting his $25 million the next day. He would not guess that his location was known.

Forte slowly shucked out the shells in his shotgun. He reinserted them in a different order so that a lead-shot cartridge would be the first shell fired, followed by two of the non-lethal shells filled with rubber balls. Then four more lethal loads if the kidnapper forced the issue. Forte hoped it wouldn't come to that, but he had no reservation about using them if he had to. In his mind it was clear: the girl's life depended on him.

He checked his watch. A quarter of an hour had passed since their last check-in. It was nearly 2 a.m.

"Forte at checkpoint two," he said into his microphone. "Moving to checkpoint number one."

"Roger that," said Nomad in his earphone.

Forte crouched and ran with his back bent as low as he could get. Running behind a row of azaleas, he dashed for the corner of the house then stopped, listening. He sprinted along the back of the house, hugging the wall as he passed below the dark windows. He stooped next to the small porch at the back door of the house.

"Forte at checkpoint one. Hold steady now," he whispered.

"Roger."

He could picture Nomad carefully taking out the flash-bang grenade and crouching under the window of the bedroom.

Forte let his breath go in and out steadily. He stayed perfectly still and let his eyes scan the back yard for any movement.

No lights had come on in any of the houses around him. Nothing moved.

He slowly swung his weapon up and pointed it at the door. One blast would do the trick.

"Engage on three," he said.

"Roger."

"One…"

Forte rose from his crouch slightly.

"…two…"

He locked his arm next to his side so that sharp recoil of the shotgun would not twist his wrist.

"… three!"

He pulled the trigger. Boom! The blast of the shotgun was almost drowned by the bigger crashing explosion of the stun grenade inside the house.

As always happened in combat, everything slowed down now. A split second was played out in what seemed like an hour.

The wood around the door lock on the back door splintered. Forte immediately smashed open the door and charged inside. He darted through the den and down a short hallway.

The door to the bedroom was open. He dived through it and came out of the roll with his shotgun leveled.

The figure was still sitting in the desk chair in front of the computer.

Usually a stun grenade put a person on the ground with hands pressed over eardrums burst or temporarily deafened by the blast.

Blam! He heard Nomad kick open the other bedroom door down the hallway. "The girl's not here," Nomad said in his earpiece.

In the houses across the street, lights blinked on behind the windows.

The figure at the desk did not move..

"Hands up!" Forte shouted.

Still no movement.

He inched to his left and pulled out his mini-light. He shined it on the man's face in the darkened room.

But it wasn't a man.

It was a plastic blow-up dummy.

From the corner of his eye, he saw a red flashing light.

"Nomad! It's a trap. Get out now!" he screamed.

\* \* \*

The killer watched the whole operation from his van parked a quarter mile away in a convenience store parking lot.

Good clean operation. Quick entry. Timed perfectly. The cameras he left behind caught it all. Couldn't have done better myself, he thought. He watched Forte slowly circle the dummy he had left in the desk chair. He just wished he could clearly see the look of surprise on the man's face. If only he had had more warning, he could have rigged a microphone to catch what the men were saying. Their last words.

He fingered the button on the remote. The red button.

Come on, now. I need the two of you together in that room.

He slowly let out his breath. He glanced over at Hallee sitting in the corner of the van. She glared at him above her gag, her eyes full of fury at being rousted from a sound sleep in the middle of the night. It couldn't be helped.

He looked back at the monitor. Forte was gone from the room.

He pressed the button.

BAHLOOM! He was surprised how loud the explosion sounded from where he sat, inside the van.

The monitor in front of him showed only static now.

He looked at the girl. Her eyes showed fear.

He stepped close to her and took the gag out of her mouth.

"Shhhh," he said. "It will be fine. It had to be done."

He moved to the driver's seat of the van and started the ignition. He doubted that Forte and his friend could have gotten far enough away to escape the blast. It had to be done.

He regretted having to get out of the house. It was a good hideaway. But regret never helped any situation.

Tomorrow the whole operation would be over and he could leave this area.

The first thing he needed to do was paint the van.

\* \* \*

The explosion decimated the room where the dummy had been seated in the desk chair. It was as if a giant claw had reached down and snatched the entire corner of the house away. A few wall studs were still attached at the floor plate of the room but the rest were fragmented and lying in the front and side yards. The roof over the room was gone.

For several seconds after the blast, pieces of shingles and tar paper rained down through the tree limbs. A car alarm across the street from the house squawked like a blackbird annoyed at being disturbed.

Forte and Nomad lay on the other side of the heavy wooden fence in the back yard. They had barely cleared it before the bomb went off.

Forte sat up. His ears rang but he was okay. Nomad sat up and shook his head. He gave Forte the OK sign.

Forte jerked his thumb toward the van. They leaped up and ran to the vehicle.

Lights were on everywhere in the neighborhood now.

The men jumped into the van. Nomad chuckled. "Quite a little party we got going on," he said.

Forte started the van and screeched out of the driveway. He shook his head to stop the buzzing in his ears. Must keep focused, keep going. To Nomad he said, "The kidnapper won't be in this neighborhood but he had to be fairly close to explode that bomb." At least three different types of sirens sounded in the distance. Police and firetrucks and ambulances would be blocking the roads of the residential neighborhood in minutes. His ears were clearing up now.

Forte steered the van out of the neighborhood until he reached an intersection with a larger thoroughfare. He mentally flipped a coin to go left or right. He took a right. This would take him closer to Highway 90. The killer would take that road if he were going to cross the river and travel north away from New Orleans.

Driving about 10 miles per hour under the speed limit, he looked at the left side of the road while Nomad searched the right side. Service stations, a fast food restaurant, an appliance repair place. He slowed as he approached a used car lot.

Three vans were on the lot. He pulled through the lot. None of them matched the description Aguilar had given him.

A police car shot past the lot, followed by an ambulance.

"Need to be moving out," Nomad said, his face still pointing to the right. "Lotta heat coming."

Forte said nothing. He pounded the steering wheel with his fist. "They're close. I know it."

He pulled out of the parking lot and drove half a block to a stop light. He waited for a the light to turn.

A van crossed in front of him. A beige van with "Nance Plumbing" on the side.

"Bingo," said Nomad.

*　*　*

The man in the beige van kept his speed steady as the emergency vehicles careened around the corner. The traffic was light and there was no need to call attention to himself.

All he had to do was make it across the bridge.

He checked his rearview mirror. A black van was behind him, keeping a couple of cars between them. He changed lanes. The black van changed lanes. *Could it be…?*

He revved his speed up and passed two cars ahead of him, then pulled over to the far right lane again and slowed. He checked his mirror.

The black van had accelerated and matched his move. It made no attempt to get closer, keeping the same distance behind him.

It's got to be Forte, he thought. *How did he find me?*

He approached a traffic light just before getting on Highway 90 which would take him across the river. He stopped and waited as a firetruck turned the corner to his right and came charging through the light in front of him. Just stay cool.

*　*　*

Forte watched the van. He hoped to keep out of sight and trail the kidnapper as long as he could before a confrontation developed.

He remembered the e-mail message he had seen from the kidnapper on the Lamberth computer. *If you want to see Hallee again,* the message had said. *For the child's sake...* There was no actual death threat. He believed that the kidnapper did not plan to kill the girl.

But he didn't want to force the issue in a rolling gun fight through the streets of New Orleans. He would keep his distance and hope to follow the killer back to his secondary hideout. A man as meticulous in his operation as this one would be sure to have one.

He seemed like a cop, Benny had said. The skinny counterfeiter would have a feel for that, for sure.

Forte glanced over at Nomad. He seemed as relaxed as if they were going for a Sunday drive through the countryside. The shotgun across his lap spoiled the effect a little.

The light changed ahead and the beige van approached the Greater New Orleans Bridge which spanned the river. He increased speed to keep up as they ramped up onto the bridge, which not only rose above the river but curved to the right as it carried traffic to and from the Big Easy. The two vans rose higher and higher as the road inclined, the bridge spans rushing past them.

A blue Ford Taurus and old maroon Nissan Stanza separated the two vans. The Ford was driven by an old man who clutched the wheel with both hands. He could not seem to decide which lane to choose. Forte watched the old man and the beige van at the same time. His speed was approaching 70 miles per hour.

Suddenly the beige van surged ahead.

Forte swerved right to get around the Ford. The old man, finally seeing the black van behind him, pulled right to try and get out of the way.

Forte jerked the wheel left at the same time the man did. The beige van was pulling away. The top of the bridge approached.

Forte pulled all the way over to the left. He floored the accelerator. The outside mirror on his door was inches from the guard rail. He could feel the warning of the speed bumps under the tires.

He was past the cars now. Eighty miles per hour. Eighty-five. The beige van had disappeared around the curve of the bridge. He was running for it.

Not good, Forte thought.

He increased speed. Ninety, ninety-five. He could see the van ahead but the kidnapper had put some space between them.

He whooshed past three other cars and a truck on the right.

The end of the bridge was closer now.

Forte gripped the wheel and leaned forward.

As the beige van zoomed off the bridge, it looked as if it would keep going straight on Highway 90 and bypass the downtown district.

At the last second, it swerved off the exit ramp.

Forte followed, feeling the centrifugal force pushing him against his door.

The kidnapper skidded left, away from the downtown area. He straightened up and gunned the van ahead. Forte stayed close, gaining ground when the chase led around corners but falling behind slightly when the beige van surged forward in the straight-aways. Under its beat-up body, the kidnapper's old van obviously had a super-charged engine.

The chase screeched through a section of burned-out warehouse buildings and excavation sites. Piles of rubble and broken bricks lay between the charred remains of textile mills and warehouses where cotton bales long ago had waited their turn to be loaded on riverboats just blocks away.

Ahead of the beige van, Forte could see a group of teenagers standing in the street, a block or two before the railroad tracks. A skinny boy shimmied to the sounds of the jambox on his shoulder.

The beige van bore down on them. One of the girls nervously edged toward the curb. The boys just slouched and looked at the approaching van.

The kidnapper kept going.

At the last possible second, the teens dived out of the street.

As Forte whooshed past them he saw the blurred glow of their cigarettes. He could hear a brief snatch of loud cursing and he was past them.

The sounds of the teenagers' voices were suddenly drowned out by the horn blast of a freight train.

The train surged along the tracks at the end of the road two blocks ahead.

The beige van barreled straight toward it.

Just when it seemed he would ram the train, the kidnapper whipped right along an access road next to the tracks. For a frozen moment, it looked as if the beige van would tip over as it skidded, the right wheels off the ground. Finally it straightened up, landed back on all four wheels and sped along in the same direction the train was moving.

Forte followed. He could see the locomotive a hundred yards ahead.

He slammed the accelerator to the floor.

The beige van was pulling even with the locomotive.

Even through his closed window, Forte could hear the clatter of the train wheels just feet away.

The beige van pulled ahead of the locomotive.

Above the din, Forte heard Nomad's voice next to him. "Oh, hell. The crazy bastard's gonna try it!"

Forte was dead-even with the train engine now.

The beige van was thirty yards ahead of it.

A crossing was ahead.

The train whistle shrieked in Forte's ear.

Ahead of him, the beige van veered toward the crossing.

It ramped upward and left the ground, sailing through the air over the tracks, the locomotive missing its back bumper by inches.

The train whistle seemed angrier as the freight cars clattered away from the crossing.

Forte skidded to a stop in a cloud of dust.

Through the gaps in the passing train cars, he could see the beige van speeding away.

He leaned back and rubbed his temples with his fingertips.

# Chapter 25

*Monday, 9:30 a.m.*

"Another beautiful spring day. Birds chirping, flowers blooming, you sitting here moping like a bump on a log." Verna Griffey had brought a mug of coffee into the office. She set it on the desk and picked up an empty mug.

Forte shifted in the desk chair where he reclined practically full length behind the desk. A New Orleans Saints cap rode low over his eyes. His arms were crossed and his legs were propped on the corner of the desk. A small television on the shelf in the corner was on with the volume turned down.

All morning, a headache had pounded the inside of his skull. Back at the treatment center, they'd called it a dry hangover – when your body experienced the effects of a binge without actually having used drugs. A number of things could trigger it: lack of sleep, excessive stress, a traumatic event, an emotional high or low. Pick one of the above, Forte thought. He tilted his head back and opened his eyes. Verna was still standing there.

"You okay?" she said.

Forte pushed the cap above his eyes. He reached for the coffee cup.

"Compared to what," he said.

"Bad night?" Verna asked.

"Something like that." He sipped the coffee and let out a long "Ahhhhhhh." Nectar of the gods.

Forte watched the TV screen. He could feel Verna's attention on his face like a heat lamp.

"You hear about that house blowing up over in Gretna?" she asked.

"Yeah," he said, still looking at the television. "It was just on the news."

"But you know nothing about it," she said.

"The house blowing up?"

"The house blowing up."

He looked directly at her now.

Verna Griffey was one of the few people who could penetrate his emotional shield. After the death of his wife, Forte had built walls between himself and anyone who came close to wanting to help him. It had taken years to repair some of the relationships he had wrecked. Some of them were beyond fixing. The walls came down slowly.

Verna and Archie were among the handful of people who had stuck with him, visiting him in treatment when he had earned the right to have visitors, calling him every few days to check his progress. Verna had taken care of his cat during his stay at the center, griping the whole time about the black hairs Boo left everywhere and the tomato plants he had dug up at her house.

When Forte had decided to start his own security firm, Verna had been the one to set up his file system and had taken over most of the details of establishing the office. She did it without asking. "With the kids grown up, I'd go crazy laying around that house listening to Archie talk about the Saints and his new fishing poles," she had said. She was a fixture around the office now and was one of the few people with password approval to get into all areas of the shelter and Forte's apartment as well. She had put herself in charge of most of the details of Forte's life and he had not complained.

Of course, at times, she did enough complaining for both of them. She knew exactly which lines, however, were not to be crossed.

She stood at the corner of the desk now watching him, the coffee mug dangling from a large black finger. "So, you don't know a thing about it then," she said.

He sipped his coffee and looked away. "Sometimes it is best that you don't know everything I know." He said it kindly and she recognized it so.

"True," she said. "So be it." She looked at him quizzically then turned and walked out of the office.

He reached over for the TV remote and clicked through the stations as he waited for the news again. Talk shows and infomercials were on almost every channel. Rarely was he forced to watch television on weekday mornings and now he remembered why he was grateful for that. Stress formula pills that worked miracles, miracle cleaners that handled everything short of nuclear waste, skin cream that miraculously erased cellulite and stretch marks, miracle stop-smoking tapes – he stopped and watched that for ten seconds then kept clicking – a mother and daughter slap-fighting over their common boyfriend, two transvestites in court over disputed costs for some kind of operation, a TV preacher with an arch of hair that started a half-inch above one ear and swept over the top of his head to the other ear.

He clicked back to the news.

An anchorwoman with perfect skin and flawless hair was delivering an update on the Gretna explosion. The screen cut to a reporter standing across the street while the camera panned past the cop cars and fire-trucks in front of the house. The mangled hole where the bomb had exploded was barely visible between the emergency vehicles at the curb.

"Police are still investigating the bombing in this peaceful neighborhood in Gretna," the reporter said. "FBI explosives experts were brought in about 3 a.m., shortly after the explosion that broke several windows in nearby houses. Authorities have ruled out a gas leak or water heater explosion as causes for the blast but are still uncertain what may have caused it. No suspects have been identified." Cut to the reporter in his blue blazer and rep tie holding a microphone in front of a fireman. "We got here quick so there wasn't much danger of a fire spreading. If anyone would have been in there, though," the fireman jerked his head toward the house, "they'd be done for now."

Forte drank his coffee and let the reporter's words drone on. It had been a close call last night, but he had had plenty of close calls in his days as a Navy SEAL and as a security consultant. What bothered him was that the kidnapper had gotten away. Forte felt the anger coming up from a deep place where it had lain seething since he had watched the beige van fly over the railroad tracks. He needed an hour or two with the punching bag before he would be able to get rid of that kind of anger. Even then, it wouldn't go away completely until he had found the kidnapper and recovered Hallee.

He didn't fool himself any more about the purity of his motives for wanting to recover the kidnapped child. He knew it wasn't just because he wanted the child to be safe. His pride was wrapped up in it. He had learned that about himself. And he knew that at the end of the day, all he could be responsible for was that he had done the best he could do toward completing his mission.

Somehow this situation was different. It was personal. And, in his business, taking things personally could get people killed.

He wondered who the kidnapper was and where he was right now.

The newscaster interrupted his thoughts. "This just in... a ransom note has been received by the Lamberth family concerning the kidnapping of Hallee Lamberth. Sources close to the FBI investigation tell us the kidnapper e-mailed the ransom note an hour ago with a demand of $25 million dollars in exchange for the 11-year-old girl." A photo of Hallee standing on the deck of a sailboat quickly cut to video footage of the Lamberth house. The newscaster continued. "The FBI's investigation of the kidnapping has produced no further leads as to the whereabouts of the kidnapper. Dr. Lamberth's father, Thomas Lamberth, has said he will pay the ransom for the return of his granddaughter."

A knock on the door drew his focus away from the television.

Rosalind Dent opened the door and closed it behind her without saying anything. She sat in the guest chair in front of his desk and laid her FBI notebook on her lap.

"Come on in, Agent Dent," Forte said. "Coffee? You look like you could use some perking up." He hit the off button on the TV remote and the television screen went black.

The FBI agent shook her head. "Where were you last night?"

Forte forced his face into calmness. He took a slow drink from his mug. He could see that the agent's eyes were bloodshot. They were locked on his face. He wondered if his lack of sleep showed under his own eyes as badly. "I was with a friend. At a bar. Why do you ask?"

"At a bar? You don't drink."

"Wasn't drinking."

"Can your friend vouch for your whereabouts?"

"Yes, but you better have a warrant in your hand when you ask him."

The air in the room seemed ten degrees cooler. Forte kept his gaze steady, as did Dent. Neither person blinked.

"I got a call this morning at 5:30 a.m. I had just gotten back into bed after a little trip over to Gretna in the middle of the night. It was a woman's voice. She said you had something to do with that explosion."

Forte felt a tiny buzz inside his head. "She called me by name?"

Dent nodded.

"And you believe her?"

The FBI agent kept her eyes steady on his. "She said we would probably find some of the neighbors around the bombed house who would say they saw a black van leaving the area right after the explosion."

Forte kept silent.

"And guess what?" Dent said. "We did find some people who saw a black van." Her eyes seemed redder now. "You drive a black van, don't you?"

"Yes."

"And, let's just say we found a witness who had written down the tag number of the van leaving the area. Could you guess what that number would be?"

Forte did not blink. "Do you have a witness?"

The agent's eyes bore into his. She had leaned forward in her chair. A moment of silence passed between them.

She leaned back. "No."

Forte let the corner of his mouth twitch. "Then I could not begin to guess what the tag number would be."

"Of course," the agent said, "we could always go door to door with your van and ask if they had seen it."

"And waste a lot of time that could better be spent finding the kidnapper," Forte said.

"Dammit, Forte," the agent hissed, "I told you to stay away from this case now. I didn't make that decision but you know that I will enforce it."

Forte drank the last of his coffee.

The phone rang. Forte picked it up.

"Forte."

The voice on the other end was unmistakable. "I just got your message from yesterday, Mr. Forte," said Jason Hamilton, "and I believe I might have an answer for you. Are you alone?"

Forte felt the FBI agent's eyes on him. "No," he said.

"Then I will talk and you listen," the pastor said. "But let me remind you that you never heard this from me. Understood?"

"Yes," Forte said as he doodled on a legal pad on his desk. "Hold for a second." He put his hand over the receiver. "Telephone survey," he said to Dent. "Just a sec."

To Hamilton he said, "Continue."

Hamilton's rich voice rolled through the wires. "There is a man, he used to be a policeman in Chicago. He was fired from the force there for refusing to arrest a pro-life protester during a demonstration. That was about a year and a half ago. Since then he has been hanging around some of the groups that the FBI calls pro-life terrorists.

"About seven months ago, he dropped out of sight, my sources tell me. One of my sources did receive a postcard from him, about the time he disappeared. It was from a place in the Caribbean. Anyway, he is the only one who matches your criteria: an ex-cop who hasn't been around recently."

Forte waited. "Yes…"

Hamilton's low chuckle came through the line. "Ah, you want his name. It is Jerah Schein." He spelled the name. "He has blond hair, very blond, almost white, cut short. I'm sure you can find out everything else you need to know about him." Hamilton paused. "I hope this helps you, Mr. Forte. I hope it helps you find the girl."

"Yes," Forte said. "Thank you for calling." He hung up.

The FBI agent stood up. "You are definitely polite to telemarketers." She eyed him suspiciously.

Forte smiled. "That's me. Mr. Polite."

# Chapter 26

*Monday, 10 a.m.*

"May I serve you?" The drive-through speaker crackled with interference.

Jerah Schein leaned out the driver's window of the van. He spoke to the speaker. "Large coffee, large orange juice, two of the eggs-and-sausage specials, two cinnamon rolls."

"Skraaak... else for you today?" the speaker said.

"That's all," Schein said.

"Your total will be... skreeeek... forward... sssss." The speaker hissed and went quiet.

Schein edged the van forward, paid for the food, and put the bags of breakfast on the floor. The engine of the van gave a deep purr as he pulled out onto the street of the small town. He listened. When he had put the high-powered engine in the old van, right after he bought it, he wondered if he would need all that power. Now he was glad for that decision.

The vehicle gave a few more creaks and groans after the flying leap over the railroad tracks the previous night. Nothing serious though. Months earlier, right after he bought the van, he had reinforced its frame and installed extra-heavy-duty shocks.

In the past few hours, he had relived the chase several times in his mind. It had been close. Very close. The blasting train horn. The wide-eyed engineer in the locomotive. The steel-on-steel clatter of the train wheels carrying hundreds of tons. The hurtling jump over the tracks. He had felt like he could reach out and touch the front of the locomotive. Then the jolt of the landing and the adrenaline rush pouring over him like a drug high.

He had driven north away from New Orleans, steering the van through the darkness of the countryside until he came to the shack in the woods. The padlock was still locked on the door of the shack. There had been no signs of tampering. The blue Pinto was still parked inside. He had pulled the van behind the shack and had checked Hallee for bruises from the car chase. After bumping her arm against the inside wall of the van when they landed after the train crossing jump, she had cried a bit. But nothing serious. They had both dozed for a few hours until the bright Louisiana sun filtered through the trees around the shack.

Now, Schein steered the van off the highway outside town and wound his way through the gravel roads. Three cows raised their heads and gave him a lazy glance as he passed, then resumed their grazing. He saw no one as he drove through the countryside.

At the shack he parked and unlocked the door. He walked around the Pinto and opened the door. Hallee lay across the back seat of the car, still asleep. He poked her with a finger.

She mumbled something and turned over on her side. He poked her again.

"Go away," she croaked.

"Breakfast is served," Schein said. He turned and walked out into the sunshine where the van was parked next to the old shack.

He opened the side door of the van and spread the food out on the built-in counter top beneath the wall-mounted monitors. He opened the lid of his coffee and drank.

Hallee climbed through the door and sat on a stool at the counter. Her hair was stuck out at a 90-degree angle from her head on the left side. She sat and looked at the food for a moment before reaching for the orange juice.

Schein put out a hand. "Shall we say grace?"

The girl blinked and stared at him.

He bowed his head. "Dear Lord, thank you for this food and all your blessings to us. Amen." He looked over at Hallee. "You didn't say grace at your house?" Inside he winced. He didn't mean to ask the question in the past tense, as if those days were over. Then again, he thought, in some ways they were gone. Forever.

Hallee popped the plastic lid off the orange juice and took two big swallows. She wiped her mouth with the back of her hand, then looked at him again. Schein could see pain in her eyes.

"Did you kill my dad?" she asked. Her eyes were filled with tears.

Schein held a piece of scrambled egg on his fork halfway between the Styrofoam plate and his mouth. He put it down.

"Yes," he said.

Hallee let out an involuntary gasping sob. "Why?"

Schein looked away from the girl. He felt sadness for her, not because of what he had done to her father but because she was forcing him to tell her some hard truth at such a young age.

"Do you know what your father did? For a living?" he asked.

She sniffed. "He was a doctor."

"Hallee, you know what he did. As a doctor."

"He performed abortions."

"And you understand what that means?"

"Yes, he helped women who didn't need children in their lives ..."

Schein interrupted. "Hallee, do you hear yourself? You said it. Children. They were children."

"But they weren't born yet..."

"They never had a chance to be born."

Hallee was silent. She reached for a napkin and blew her nose.

"But the women," she said, her voice low, "they chose to do it, not my father."

Schein had heard it before. He felt sorry for the girl. She had believed a lie so young.

"He helped them kill their children, Hallee. It's hard to hear but it is true. I had to stop him."

She looked at him now, her eyes a mixture of pain and anger in the dim light of the van.

"Then you are no better than you say he was. You murdered him."

"I saved children's lives."

She sniffed again but her tears were gone now. "You had no right."

Schein was quiet now. He picked up his fork and ate another bite of the eggs. He would not debate the girl about the issue. After all, her father was dead. He tossed the plastic fork into the disposable tray and snapped shut the tray lid. He was suddenly not hungry. He picked up both of their trays and motioned for her to follow him.

"You can eat outside somewhere. I need to shut the doors to the van," he said.

She took her food and sat under a tree close to the shack.

Schein stepped inside and found the masking tape, old newspapers, buckets of paint and primer, and the paint sprayer. He set everything on the ground next to the van, then went back inside the shed and brought out a gasoline-operated generator. He yanked the cord to start the generator. It took two pulls but it started up. The sound of the generator was loud in the woods. Schein welcomed the noise.

He shut it off and picked up the tape. He carefully taped the windows, bumpers, door handles, grillwork and chrome mirrors on the old van. Every minute or so, he glanced over at the tree where Hallee sat sipping on her juice with her head against the tree trunk.

As he walked around the end of the van to tape the fixtures on the other side, he caught a movement from the corner of his eye. Hallee had waited until she thought he was out of sight before jumping up and running through the woods.

Schein walked back around the van and set the tape down. He watched her run for a moment. Then he trotted after her.

With the sunshine playing through the new spring leaves, the morning revived his spirits as he jogged along. The girl had sprinted out to a quarter mile distance but he knew that they were miles away from any house. She would soon tire.

Slowly he gained on her. A hundred yards away, then fifty, then ten. He could hear her gasping for breath. Before he could reach her, she stumbled and fell to the leafy carpet in the woods. He stood over her, breathing easily.

Hallee's breath was coming in great gulps as she lay there. She put up a hand as if to fend him off.

Schein stopped and leaned against a tree, his breathing faster but still steady. The day would be humid, he could tell. He wiped a trickle of sweat off his forehead.

"No," Hallee rasped. "I don't want to go."

"You have to," said Schein.

Hallee sat up. Her breath came a little easier now.

Her face was twisted in fear. "Are you going to kill me too?"

Schein looked at her. If she only knew...

"No," he said. "You will be fine if everything comes together like it should."

He held out a hand to help the girl up. She looked at his hand then stood up without taking it.

He shrugged. "Back to the van," he said. "If you try that again, I will tie you up and gag you again."

Hallee said nothing. Her face was streaked with tears and dust. Leaves and twigs were stuck in her hair.

Back at the shack, he quickly finished taping the fixtures. He plugged the paint sprayer into the generator, then jerked the cord to start it up. The racket of the motor took his mind away from the girl's accusations.

He really couldn't expect her to understand.

# Chapter 27

*Monday, 2 p.m.*

With its green painted walls and metal desks, the Chicago police precinct looked like any other government office. The difference was that these city employees carried guns.

"How long did Schein work in your department?" Forte asked the lean man with the brush cut on the other side of the desk.

Captain Stephen Taylor sat with his hands folded across his chest and thought for a moment. "I'd say... about three-and-a-half years." He brushed a piece of lint off his jacket. "And he did a great job. He was probably the best man I had in a high-risk situation. He just went bonkers there at the end."

"How so?"

"He began talking about the abortion doctors, how they were killing babies." Taylor shrugged. His shoulders were those of a man who could still be leading the Chicago SWAT team if he hadn't been promoted to precinct chief. "Because he was on the SWAT team, he wasn't assigned to that kind of duty, guarding the abortion clinics. But he began doing volunteer stuff with the abortion protestors, making sure that if a fight came up between the pro-life people and the pro-choice guys, that his side didn't come out on the short end.

"The final straw came when he was part of the team sent in to rescue a group of hostages at a clinic. The so-called pro-life terrorists were not armed but they had bopped a couple of the clinic's escorts. We sprayed them all down with tear gas and dragged the hostage-takers out onto the street. Schein refused to participate. Disobeyed a direct order. I hated to do it, but I had to can him."

On the captain's desk was a grouping of photos in stand-up frames. Some family photos of him and his wife and two teenage daughters, another of him 20 years younger in dress blues, and one of him and Schein and an older man.

Forte pointed to the picture. "May I?"

Taylor nodded.

The man in the picture had his arm around Schein's shoulder. A sailboat floated in the distant background of the photo. Forte wondered if the older man was Schein's father. The little that he had found on Schein on the Internet had to do with some national SWAT team competitions he had won and a couple of pro-life web pages that listed the man as a consultant for "rescues of the unborn."

Taylor took the picture back from Forte. He pointed at the white-haired man in the photo. "This is Father Tim Buell. He was the headmaster at the orphanage where Jerah grew up. The only dad he ever knew."

"He's here in Chicago?" Forte asked.

"Yeah, he's in the book."

"You do some sailing?"

"Yeah. We used to sail a lot together, Jerah and me. Some good times, believe it or not. He was a loyal guy. It killed me to have to fire him."

The phone rang and the police captain answered it. "No, tell him that insurance won't kick in again for 30 days." He paused. "Good. Take care of it." He hung up. "Paperwork and personnel stuff. It's mostly what I do now." His brows were lowered over his eyes as he looked at Forte. "This stuff about Jerah Schein. You are pretty sure he was involved in the Lamberth business?"

"Yeah," Forte said. "Pretty sure. Does that surprise you?"

Taylor looked thoughtful. "Nothing surprises me any more after 20 years as a cop. Jerah was a friend, but he had his dark moments. I can see him doing some pretty drastic stuff if he believed it was the right thing to do." He picked up a pencil and tapped it on the desktop. "But the FBI isn't on to Schein yet, right?"

Forte was stone-faced. "Don't know. I'm not part of their investigation."

Taylor nodded. "Probably a good thing."

Forte stood up. "Yeah. All the way around."

\* \* \*

"Coffee? Tea?" asked Father Tim Buell. "A glass of red wine? I have to drink a glass a day for my cholesterol."

Forte turned from the fireplace where logs crackled. The small town of Langston north of Chicago was enduring a late cold snap. "Coffee would be good, Father."

"Just call me Tim. Be right back."

The house was small and tidy with the type of fastidious yard that people produce when they have lived most of their lives without one. Buell's career had been spent giving hope to abandoned kids in the inner city of Chicago. Forte almost regretted having to talk to him about Schein.

The white-haired man came back into the den and put a saucer and a cup of black coffee in front of Forte on the coffee table. Forte sat. Buell set down his own cup and shuffled over to a built-in bookshelf next to the fireplace. He reached up for a thick photo album, his cardigan sweater rising above his belt in the back to expose thread-bare corduroy belt loops.

"This is my book of memories," Buell said, plopping the book on the table. The coffee cups jumped at the impact. Forte held his cup steady but he could see a drop of coffee had splashed out of the old man's cup.

Buell started thumbing through the album, whispering to himself the names and events of the boys whose photos sparked his recollection. He looked up suddenly at Forte. "You say you were a friend of Jerah's?"

Forte nodded. "I was pretty close to him at one time, yes. But, sadly, I lost track of him."

Buell, still hunched over the album, pushed his wire-rim glasses up on his nose. "Yes, he is like that. You will hear from him for a while, then he drops out of sight. He was a moody boy at times."

"When did you last hear from him?"

Buell sat up and ran a hand over his forehead. "It has been quite a while ago, actually. Probably seven or eight months. He said he was going to be out of the country for a long while. Now that I think of it, it's probably been the longest time between visits."

Forte had a momentary pang of conscience at his misleading the old man. But he had to know as much as he could about Schein. "You were close."

"Yes. He was always respectful and obedient, unlike some of the boys we had at the orphanage. Jerah wanted to become a priest at one time, you know."

"Is that right?" Forte said to keep the chat moving.

"Yes, he would study the Bible and his catechisms for hours it seemed."

"How old was he when you first met him?"

"About five, I believe it was," Buell said. "His mother was, how can I say this, rather unstable. She had come to Chicago in the summer of 1968 for the protests at the Democratic Convention. She told everyone she was raped by a policeman and that was how Jerah was conceived. Forgive my bluntness, but Jerah's father could have been one of many, according to the word on the street."

Forte took a drink of coffee. "And she gave him up for adoption."

"Yes. The Department of Human Services actually took Jerah away from her. She just drifted in the streets, even when the church and others tried to help her. She was arrested several times for drugs and finally died of an overdose the year after Jerah came to the orphanage." Buell took off his glasses and polished them with the hem of his sweater. "I believe she knew she was doomed and wanted to make a safe place for her son. It was her most selfless act for the boy by far."

Forte let the information sink in. He could relate to feeling adrift as a child. "What was he like, his hobbies, any activities…"

"Oh, he was a good student. In fact, he was probably harder on himself than anyone else, his teachers or coaches included. He was an outstanding athlete in basketball and baseball. What he really loved was sailing, a hobby of mine, too."

"You have a boat?"

"I had a 22-foot Catalina that we took out on Lake Michigan in the summers. We had a grand time."

"Did you ever sail anywhere else?"

Buell stopped thumbing through the album. "No, but it's funny you should ask." He leaned back and sipped his tea. "When Jerah was young, the church youth group went to Central America on mission trips for two or three weeks at a time. Jerah loved it there. Belize was where we spent most of our time. He always said he would love to sail a big boat all the way down there." Buell had a faraway look on his face.

Forte felt a buzz. "Do you know if he ever got to do it?"

"No, I don't know if he did. But it wouldn't surprise me a bit if he made it there. He usually accomplished what he set out to do."

"No," said Forte, "it wouldn't surprise me either."

# Chapter 28

*Monday, 5:15 p.m.*

Forte slumped against the pay phone at Chicago's O'Hare International Airport, watching the crowds of people hurry past him while he was on hold. A pair of flight attendants smiled at him as they passed.

The on-hold music on the phone stopped abruptly. A woman's voice came through the phone line. "Jon Brach is out of the office at the moment. May I take a message?"

"No," said Forte. "I'll check back."

He hung up and walked over to the seating area where he had been waiting for his flight back to New Orleans. He had been calling in throughout the day, hoping to hear that Hallee had been released. No word yet.

Forte knew he had done everything in his power to get the girl back. That certainty, however, failed to erase his vague sense of failure at how things had turned out. He closed his eyes and listened to the airport sounds around him.

Within two minutes he got up again and went back to the bank of phones on the wall. He punched in a long-distance code and waited. Jackie Shaw picked up.

"Hi. How are you feeling?" he asked.

"Like I was thrown down on concrete and shot in the leg," she said. "Actually I'm doing fine. The doctor got out the shotgun pellets. Two of them. They were fairly close to the surface. He told me to take it easy for a few days."

Forte listened. She had done a good job holding off the attackers the night before. Was it only yesterday?

"Any word from the District Attorney's office about releasing Kyra?" he asked.

"An assistant D.A. took the confession from the guy who shot up the van, the one who turned himself in. The man said he was not directed by Ricardo Aguilar to attack the shelter. He was vague about exactly who gave him the orders. But the D.A. will probably sign the order to release Kyra to her grandmother's care pretty soon."

"Good," said Forte.

The line was silent.

"What?" he said.

"Oh, nothing," Jackie said.

"Nothing?" Forte could feel the effect of the sleep deprivation.

"Well, you sound tired. Is everything okay?" She did not ask him where he was or what he was doing out of town.

He rubbed his eyes. When he opened them, a small boy was walking past. He stuck his tongue out at Forte.

"Al?"

Forte shifted the phone to his other ear. "Yeah, it's been a fun-filled weekend, hasn't it? I just need some more sleep. I'll check in later." They said goodbyes and he hung up.

Forte checked his watch. Another hour until his flight went out. He walked around the corner to a lounge, ordered a Coke, and asked the bartender to change the TV channel to CNN. A commercial for Internet stock trading flashed across the screen.

He thought about Schein and what he knew about him. The guy had a difficult start in life but a lot of people had overcome worse beginnings. He was a star athlete who had earned attention for his victories. Schein showed evidence of wanting to do the right thing, according to Father Buell. His will and discipline had produced a determination that usually allowed him to reach the goals he set for himself. He had believed that murdering the doctor was the right thing. He had believed he was saving lives.

How did the kidnapping of Hallee Lamberth fit in? Somehow the profile of Schein didn't match up with someone who would threaten a child in order to get money.

Would Schein really hurt her? Or was he bluffing?

From what he had heard, Hallee's grandparents were not taking the chance of finding out. His reporter friend Brach had told him earlier that the ransom money from the Lamberth family was ready to be transferred to the offshore account before noon today.

The commercial was over. The smile was gone from the anchorwoman's face as she read from the teleprompter. "CNN has just learned that Hallee Lamberth, the kidnapped daughter of murdered abortion doctor Tyson Lamberth, was not released to her family today. The ransom money, however, had already been transferred to an offshore bank account before authorities discovered that the duffel bag that was supposed to contain Hallee Lamberth was stuffed with pillows." The woman continued reading the news.

"FBI spokesperson Rosalind Dent confirmed the failure of authorities to recover the girl." The screen cut to Rosie Dent standing in a wooded area. "The kidnapper claimed to have a high-power rifle trained on the duffel bag and threatened to shoot if the money was not transferred. The FBI advised the Lamberth family to wait on the money transfer but the family decided not to take that risk." The dark areas had deepened under the FBI agent's eyes since Forte had seen her that morning.

The screen cut back to the anchorperson. "Freida Lamberth, mother of the kidnapped girl and widow of Tyson Lamberth, has been hospitalized and treated with sedatives after hearing the news." The news moved on to other things.

Forte realized he was on his feet as he watched the news report. He didn't remember getting up from the padded booth where his soft drink sat on the table. He picked up the drink and drained it, then walked back out into the vast space of the waiting area. He walked all the way over to the wall of 30-foot windows that overlooked a runway.

*Hallee's gone. The kidnapper's gone. The money's gone.*

*And here I am looking up at the sky in Chicago.*

# Chapter 29

*Monday, 11 p.m.*

The house looked lonely without any cars in the driveway or policemen patrolling the wall. Then again, Forte thought, with Freida Lamberth resting in the hospital there was no one left at home for anyone to guard.

He just hoped they had not changed the code on the security systems. There were two alarm systems to worry about, one at the gate and one to get into the house itself.

Forte had parked his van a quarter-mile away and had spent a half hour jogging through the Garden District in a bright blue windsuit. He had passed the Lamberth house a half-dozen times from different directions, scrutinizing every angle of the house for signs of movement. He had seen no movement in or around the house.

The seventh time he approached the house, he slowed as he neared the security gate at the driveway. He scanned the street. No other runners or dog-walkers or cyclists were out. He stopped at the gate. Quickly he punched in the security code from memory. He stopped with his hand on the gate handle. Clack, whirrr. The gate swung open.

Forte stepped through quickly and hit the Close button on the control panel inside. The gate reversed direction and clicked shut. Forte stepped into the shadows next to the gate and quickly peeled off the windsuit. Underneath he was dressed in urban night camouflage, a mottled design of grays that blended with the shadows. His only weapon was his nine millimeter automatic. He was traveling light.

He crouched in the shrubbery along the wall and kept perfectly still as he watched the house for five minutes. When he was certain there was no one moving about in the house, he darted to the side door entrance. Quickly, he punched in the code on the alarm panel next to the door.

The red light next to "Armed" blinked off. He was safe.

He opened the door and went in.

Forte armed the security system again, then stood next to the door for a moment and listened for any movement. Satisfied, he took out a small but powerful flashlight and began a walk-through of the house. He wasn't quite sure what he was looking for. But he would know when he found it. Besides, he had learned long ago that when there was a problem to be solved and there seemed to be no solution, just find the tiniest thread and start tugging on it. Sometimes the whole ball of yarn would come unraveled.

The kitchen was orderly. No food or dishes had been left out. He imagined the dark-haired woman in her starched white outfit, the one who had brought the cop and him coffee, keeping busy washing cups and saucers while the household drifted in suspense waiting for Hallee's release.

He had been in dozens of homes as they waited for news, desperately hoping beyond hope for good news.

He was not much for the waiting part.

His preference for action rather than contemplation had seemed rash to some of his commanding officers. It had always been both a strong point and a weak point for him. His evaluations during SEALs training always included phrases such as "candidate borders on impatience at times during a mission" and "candidate comes close to relying more on his intuition than thoughtful planning in missions."

He remembered being discouraged when a commanding officer first shared those negative comments with him in a regularly scheduled review. After the meeting, however, the officer had read some other comments to him, off the record. "Candidate consistently proves to achieve higher success rates in the completion of mission objectives than any other man in his group. His decision-making skills in combat and his reflexes have made his strike team the most effective the training center has seen in years."

Over the years, he had accepted his skills and had learned to recognize when they were an asset or a liability. He had gradually reached the point where he was not hesitant to depend on others whose abilities complemented his.

Tonight, however, this was a one-man job.

He walked down the short hallway next to the kitchen to the first floor study where the computer had been. It was still on the desk, powered off. Forte shone his flashlight over the cables behind the computer box, looking for any detection device or alarms around the computer. Seeing none, he pushed the power button and listened to the hum of the power supply fan and the clickity-click of the computer's hard drive as it booted up.

When the operating system finished loading, he quickly double-clicked through several folders. He scanned the contents of the Temporary folder then navigated to the Temporary Internet Files folder, which indicated web sites the computer user had visited on the Internet. Most of the web sites listed seemed to fit into four categories: medical research, grade school education, fashion trends, and sailing. Nothing jumped out at him

He clicked the X button and closed the window, then opened the e-mail program. He scanned the inbox and read the ransom message from Schein. The other messages were mostly junk mail.

Forte closed the e-mail program window, then shut down the computer. He got up and walked through the rest of the rooms downstairs. Finding nothing of interest, he went up the stairs.

The door to Hallee's room was open. He went in.

Everything had been tidied up. The bed was made, the clothes picked up off the floor, the bookshelves straightened. The stuffed tiger that Hallee had been holding when he first met her was propped on the shelf of the multimedia center. Forte looked closely. The medallion with the scripture reference had been taken off the collar. Probably tagged and bagged for evidence by some of the FBI's forensic people.

Forte slowly let the flashlight travel over the shelves of the media center. Nothing leaped out at him and screamed 'This is a clue.' He edged down to the end of the built-in desk, still looking at the books and CD titles on the shelf at eye level. He idly spun the globe on the stand as he studied the shelves' contents. He turned to walk out of the room.

He turned back to the globe as it slowly stopped spinning. He leaned closer, holding the flashlight at an angle to eliminate its glare off the metal finish of the globe.

The faint ghost remained of a red X that had been marked on the globe. It looked as if it had been rubbed with some kind of cleaner in an attempt to remove the mark. The X was practically invisible if viewed straight on. But when a light was held at an angle to the sphere, it could be seen, if very faintly.

The X had been marked in the Caribbean region of the globe. Next to an island. Off the coast of Belize.

Forte stood very still. He remembered his conversation with Father Buell about Jerah Schein's dream of sailing to the Caribbean.

He pulled open the desk drawer and scooped up the dozen or so pens that lay in the tray inside the drawer. He sat at the desk, grabbed a notebook and flipped it open to a blank page. He opened each pen and scribbled on the paper. Only two of the pens wrote in red ink.

He turned to the globe and made an X with each of the red pens. None came close to the type of mark produced by the X near Belize. He took a tissue and wiped away the marks he had made.

Hallee had not made the X on the globe. Who had?

Forte got up and went up the stairs to Freida's room. Moving quickly, he rifled through the drawers of the two bedside stands. He came up with three red felt-tip pens. He ran back to the globe in Hallee's room.

He tried the first one. No match. The second. No match.

He carefully made an X with the third marker.

He looked at the faded original X. Then back to the one he had added.

It made the exact same type of mark.

Forte sat on the edge of the bed and thought it over. It was such a stretch that the FBI would not believe any of this, even if he could convince them he was not obstructing justice merely by trying to track down the kidnapper.

But it was all he had to go on.

He found the phone book in Hallee's desk, took out his cell phone, and dialed the hospital. He was connected to the nurse's station near Freida Lamberth's room. He asked to speak to the policeman at her room. A pause, then the cop came on the line.

"Officer Gordon, can I help you?"

"I need to talk to Freida Lamberth."

"She is resting now. Can't come to the phone." The cop sounded irritated. "Who is calling?"

"A friend," Forte said. "Listen, can you just do this: go into her room and see if she is okay. Please, it won't take but a second."

"Listen, man, I don't know what you ..."

"It is important. You don't have to wake her up. Just see if she is there. Please," Forte said, his voice urgent now.

The line was silent for a beat. Then the officer said, "Hold on."

Forte waited. He heard the man get up and open the door.

Almost immediately, he heard the door bang open and the guard shouted something down the hallway. The cop picked up the phone. "She's gone! Who is this..."

Forte disconnected the line.

# Chapter 30

Forte looked over at the child in the passenger seat of the van. Kyra was holding up her doll so it could look at the sights of the French Quarter as they passed by.

"See, Penelope," Kyra told the doll, "that's where the beautiful princess lives when she comes to visit. And nobody will ever ever come to hurt her."

Forte drove the van east through the narrow streets, past Jackson Square and the old French Market. Soon he was out of the official boundaries of the Quarter. The buildings were still small compared to the high-rise structures in the downtown area. They were less ornate than the renovated apartments and storefronts in the well-traveled parts of the Quarter.

He pulled a scrap of paper out of his tee-shirt pocket. The address was near. He slowed the van as he checked the numbers on the crowded apartments. He pulled to the curb in front of an apartment that was noticeably more well kept than the other homes on the narrow street.

Standing at the bottom of the stoop were Skull Cap and Goatee, the thugs he had first seen with Poochie. As the van stopped, Goatee walked up the stairs and rapped on the door with his knuckles. The door opened and Poochie walked out into the sunshine. He stepped aside and another person followed him out of the apartment.

She was an older woman in a stylish blue dress. She shaded her eyes with a hand and looked closely at the van. Forte could see the wrinkles in the old woman's coffee skin around her eyes as she recognized Kyra.

"Gran-mama!" Kyra squealed next to him. Forte got out and went around to help Kyra out. As soon as her seatbelt was unbuckled she shot out of the van and ran to the old woman who scooped her up and hugged her close.

"Kyra sweetie, my precious baby," the woman said, her eyes closed. Her voice sounded as if tears were close to the surface. She opened her eyes and saw Forte standing on the sidewalk. She mouthed the words "Thank you" soundlessly.

Poochie watched the reunion silently, a smile playing across his face. For a moment, he almost looked like a normal proud uncle, Forte thought. *Some good in the worst, some bad in the best.*

\* \* \*

Back at his office, Forte walked to the window, peered out for a few moments, then meandered back to his desk. It was his fifth trip back and forth. He was restless. He had telephoned Jon Brach at the newspaper and left a voicemail message for him. Other calls to Rosie Dent at the FBI and to other contacts in the New Orleans Police Department and Orleans Parish District Attorney's office had been fruitless. Everyone was out.

Forte sat for about five minutes at his desk, drumming a pencil on a yellow legal pad. On the pad he drew a vertical line with two headings at the top of the page: "Person/Situation" and "Disposition." He had quickly jotted down the facts to fill out the two columns:

Tyson Lamberth: Murdered by Jerah Schein

Hallee Lamberth: Kidnapped by Schein. Whereabouts – unknown.

Ransom Money: In kidnapper's bank account; offshore, untouchable.

Freida Lamberth: Disappeared. Kidnapped? Whereabouts – unknown.

Forte looked at the list. A lot had happened in the past three days. He had been hired to protect an 11-year-old girl. She had been stolen from the very house he was guarding while he was in the bedroom of the girl's mother. He had been shot at by thugs he thought were Colombians but turned out to be hired by the kidnapper. He had come within ten seconds of being blown up by a bomb after coming within minutes of finding the kidnapped girl. Now the $25 million ransom money from the Lamberth family was gone and the kidnapped girl's mother had disappeared.

"One of my finest hours," he said aloud.

About the only thing Forte knew for sure at the moment was that he was actually sitting at his desk. Come to Forte Security, the bastion of ineptitude. You can't count on us but we're good for a few chuckles to relieve your stress.

For another minute or so he beat himself up as he waited for his calls to be returned. Then he got up and walked past Verna's desk to get some coffee. A few minutes later he went back through to find the newspaper. He came through again to find another pencil.

Verna looked up from her paperwork, her eyes trailing him over the top of her reading glasses. "You might need to ease up on that coffee," she said. "Just a suggestion."

He didn't respond as he walked past.

At his desk, he picked up the pad from the desktop and walked around the room slapping it against his leg. Outside his office another bright April morning beckoned but not for him. On the streets below a few people strolled along the sidewalk, on the way to their apartments or to the Square or to the park, apparently enjoying life as worry-free as a dolphin in the sea, leaping and chattering in the sun-splashed waves.

He thought about the mark that had been rubbed away from the surface of Hallee's metal globe. It wasn't enough to tell the FBI about. But it was something.

In the next room, Verna called out to him. "You better turn on the news," she shouted.

He threw the legal pad on his desk, found the remote and clicked on the TV.

The picture showed a large sailboat looming above a Coast Guard cruiser. On the rear of the boat was the name "Tyson's Reward."

Forte turned up the volume.

"... was located by a Coast Guard rescue team an hour ago. Apparently, an SOS signal had been sent out from the radio on Lamberth's boat at 6:30 this morning. When rescuers reached the craft, they found it empty but with bloodstains on the deck." The picture cut to a shaky scene, shot from a news helicopter, that showed a man in an FBI jacket bending over a dark red stain on the boat in front of the sailboat's main cabin.

The scene cut to the news studio where a distinguished looking anchorman calmly continued. "Investigators have rushed the blood sample to their lab to determine if the blood is that of Freida Lamberth, the widow of murdered abortion doctor Tyson Lamberth. Mrs. Lamberth was discovered missing from her hospital room last night. She had been recovering from the shock of the kidnapping of her daughter, Hallee, who had been scheduled to be returned yesterday afternoon. Eleven-year-old Hallee was abducted..."

The phone rang and Verna answered. "For you," she called out.

Forte picked up.

"Are you watching the news?" asked Jon Brach.

"Yes, I saw it," Forte said.

"Here's an update that the TV people don't have yet," Brach said. Forte could hear an ambulance siren through the phone in the background. "The FBI did a quick test on the blood found at the boat. It's Freida Lamberth's."

Forte's heart sank. "Not good," he said.

"Not for her," the reporter said. "But I've got more for you."

What could be worse, Forte thought.

"The last will and testament of Tyson Lamberth was read earlier this morning. The NCLU just held a press conference. Dr. Lamberth's estate was worth 40 million bucks. He left half of his money to his daughter Hallee, forty percent to the NCLU, five percent to Tulane University. That leaves five percent to his wife. Freida got the house too." The reporter paused. "But it looks like she won't be around to enjoy it."

Forte held the phone to his ear as he looked out the window of his office.

"Al? You there?"

Forte sat down at his desk. "Yeah, I'm here. Thanks for calling me back. Strange world, isn't it?"

"Yeah, it can be at times. Gotta run now. Bye."

Forte hung up the phone. He picked up his coffee mug, looked into it, then set it back on the desk. He picked up the legal pad and looked at the list he had made.

Next to Freida Lamberth's name he marked through the word 'Kidnapped.'

He left the question mark where it was.

# Chapter 31

*Wednesday, 3:30 p.m.*

"Where have you been since yesterday?" said Verna, never one to beat around the bush. She was standing in the middle of Forte's den in his apartment, a feather duster in her hand as she watched the man come in.

"Just wandering around some, thinking," Forte said. He threw his keys on the table and went out on the balcony. Boo the cat lay on his back in the big round cushion chair in the corner. He stretched mightily as Forte approached, his yellow eyes squeezed shut, and leaped out of the way as his master fell backwards into the chair.

"One day you gonna squish that cat," said Verna. She had followed him out onto the balcony. Boo looked at her and leaped down from the back of the cushion. He rubbed himself against her legs, obviously intent on seducing her out of some cat treats.

"All right, you black panther, you," Verna said. "You know I can't resist that lovin'." She walked back into the apartment, shook some catfood into a bowl, and brought it back to the balcony. Boo purred loudly as he ate.

Verna leaned against the doorway and watched Forte. He was sprawled in the huge chair, his hands folded over his stomach and his feet propped on a low table in front of him. Like a little boy who lost a ball game, she thought.

She had known about Al Forte for years, but their relationship had been cemented through their spouses. Her husband Archie had been the liaison with the city's social workers in the Department of Housing and Neighborhood Development. He had come home talking about a young lady who had a gift for working with the inner city kids. When Al Forte had visited the precinct house during a furlough in the Navy, Archie had dropped her name. The two young people found themselves across the table at the Griffey's before they knew what hit them.

Verna smiled to herself. That Archie. The matchmaker. When Ruth had been killed by one of her own clients, he had been devastated, as had Verna. They helplessly stood by as Al spiraled downward in his drug use, unable to stop him. Their only comfort had been in each other. They vowed to be there for Forte if he ever called for help.

Those days seem like long ago now. It still hurt her to see the young man in pain, however.

She knew all about the Lamberth case. It was one of the few times that Forte Security had failed on a mission and the only time a client had been kidnapped while under Al's care. He did not like it a bit. None of them did. But that was the way it was and the best response was to move on to the next challenge.

"So," she said aloud. "You just gonna mope around here the rest of your life?"

Forte kept his eyes shut but waved a hand in Verna's direction. Boo saw the movement and jumped on his lap. "I'm thinking of taking some time off. Maybe go fishing with Larue for a few days out in the swamp." He scratched the cat's head, inducing even louder purring and a furious bout of kneading on Forte's chest.

Verna whooped and Boo's head popped up at the sudden sound. "Now that ought to be a whole big ole barrel of fun right there. You and that old man in a boat not saying a word between you for days, floating around in the God-forsaken swamp. Y'all gonna bore the alligators right outta their skins."

Forte opened one eye and looked at her. "Sometimes a little silence can be good for a soul, Verna. You should try it." He closed the eye and settled further in the cushion.

"I know when to keep my mouth shut," the black woman said, "I just seldom see a situation that could not be improved by a bit of my advice. And being the giving person that I am, I am not shy about sharing my wisdom as I see fit."

Forte laughed out loud at this last display of sassiness. Verna smiled. She had helped brighten the man's dark mood if but for a few minutes.

"So you will be gone for how long?" she asked.

"Not sure. A few days. Probably less than a week."

"It will be good for you, really." She turned to continue her housework. "Just let us know when you get back."

* * *

Jerah Schein stood on the deck of the 45-foot sailboat, his legs bent slightly as he rocked with the boat's movement through the waves. A warm breeze flowed over him as he scanned the horizon. No land in sight and no other boats anywhere. Just sun-dappled water everywhere and a blue canopy of sky overhead. He inhaled another deep lungful of the sea air in the afternoon brightness before going down into the spacious cabin of the boat.

He was still amazed and delighted at how much room the big sailboat afforded. He remembered the cramped quarters of the little boat he and Father Buell had sailed across choppy chilly Lake Michigan. Those were fun days amidst the darkness of his childhood. But this — this was paradise. With millions in the bank, he could afford to indulge himself in his one true vice – sailing. And if he had to rationalize the purchase of the boat, he could easily say it was part of his mission.

He felt a sense of peace that had eluded him for months. He had not realized it was gone until he regained it. During his mission in New Orleans he had concentrated so intently on every step of his plan, enduring months of planning before waiting until the right moment to strike.

Now it was done. He smiled. Now he could relax for a while.

He made his way to the kitchen and took the steaks out of the freezer to thaw. He would grill them later out under the stars. Perfecto.

He turned to the side of the sink. A towel lay there on the counter, folded over itself twice.

He unwrapped the towel. It was sticky with redness.

He picked up the bloody knife. Taking a steelwool pad, he ran it under a stream of hot water from the faucet, then slowly scrubbed the crusted blood from the blade.

# *Chapter 32*

*Saturday, 7:30 a.m.*

The beaches of Ambergris Caye were nearly empty at this hour, the tourists sleeping in for the most part after a busy night of partying in San Pedro Town. The island's largest town, with it's mile-long stretch of unpaved sandy streets, could more accurately be called a village. But its quaint rustic charm was the island's biggest draw. Vacationers came here with the purpose of trading a bit of convenience for the chance to get away from the high-rise buildings, traffic and billboards of their fast-paced lives.

A bum rolled over on a pillow of newspapers so he could watch from beneath the torn brim of his straw hat as the waves rolled onto the beach. The breeze coming off the Caribbean made his tattered clothes flutter and threatened to turn the hat into a kite. He put a hand up to keep the hat on his head. He had found it in a dumpster behind a hotel and he didn't want to lose it. The sea breeze had a way of disguising the heat that would bake the white sand of the island as the sun rose higher in the sky. For tourists with plenty of sunscreen and fancy beach umbrellas, the sun was another of the Belize island's attractions. For him, it could mean sunstroke, especially without a hat.

And who would rescue a smelly creature like him as he lay boiling like a lobster on the beach?

He stretched and sat up. Sand fell from his dreadlocks and cascaded down the neck of his torn sweat-stained tee-shirt. Some of the tiny grains of irritation even made it under the waistband of his threadbare khaki pants. With the movements of a man twice his age, he rolled on his side and pushed himself up on all fours, then to one knee. He peeled off the shirt and shook as much sand out of it as he could before slapping the cloth over his chest and back to dislodge more sand. A dirty Band-Aid clung to his forearm with one edge flapping. He pressed the bandage back in place.

He donned the tee-shirt and stood up. He stretched again, his arms reaching toward the deep blue above his head. Time to look for food.

The limestone coral island of Ambergris Caye stretched along the coast of Belize and paralleled the barrier reef of that small Central American country. Ambergris was a mere 25 miles in length and the habitable part was less than that. He had walked most of it. Several times.

The people of the island were friendly for the most part, chattering in Spanish among themselves but addressing the tourists in English. They generally ignored him as he shuffled along searching garbage cans behind the buildings that lined Barrier Reef Drive, San Pedro's main street.

The town was about a quarter mile down the beach. He picked up his shopping bag and shuffled in that direction. To his left, an older couple walked hand in hand along the water's edge, their heads bent to discover polished shells. The bum watched them from beneath the straw hat and tilted his head a bit more to watch a sailboat glide through the water a few hundred yards from the beach. He stopped and watched the boat for a moment, then resumed his plodding through the sand. From time to time he stopped and examined the edges of beach towels that lay half-buried in the beach, forgotten by their owners. No treasures were wrapped in the terry folds of the towels. One of them might provide him with a blanket to replace the newspapers he had been using to block the night breeze as he slept.

A golf-cart carrying a deeply tanned man of about 70 whizzed past the bum who trudged along the sand street of the town. Few people under retirement age were out and about at this hour. That was fine with him. The town police were fairly tolerant but they could get irate if he gave any appearance of pestering the tourists. This island may have been a former pirate hideout and might still claim to have a fishing industry but these days tourism was king and the powers-that-be made sure it went unimpeded.

The bum walked around to the back of a building and rummaged through a couple of cardboard boxes that had been discarded. Nothing of use here. He lifted the lid of a small blue dumpster and let the morning sun illuminate its insides. He peered in then let the lid down slowly. No loud clanging to attract the  interest of the authorities.

He kept moving from building to building, trash can to dumpster, behind the stores and souvenir shops of the island town. A worker, one of the 2000 or so Spanish-Mestizo natives of the island, came out of the back door of a restaurant ahead of him. He threw a trash bag into the dumpster and glanced at the disheveled man then went inside. The bum waited for a moment, then approached the trash bin and opened the lid. The stench of rotting food hit him in the face. He persisted, however, sorting through the bundles until he pulled out the bag the man had just discarded. Ahhh, breakfast. He pulled out two Styrofoam containers with aluminum foil bundles inside. He unwrapped the foil to reveal large slabs of grilled swordfish that had been left over from the previous night's dinner crowd. He smelled the fish then carried it over to the edge of the building. He sat and leaned against the wooden wall of the restaurant and broke off a piece of the fish with his fingers. He popped it into his mouth. Heaven.

He forced himself to chew slowly as he ate, having learned his lesson about putting too much food on an empty stomach. Sometimes a whole day would pass before he found a morsel like this one, but the rich sauces on some of the leftovers could make his insides rebel. He finished the fish and let his head rest against the building, his straw hat across his lap. He could easily fall asleep here but it was best to keep moving. If he stayed in the alley and dozed, eventually a policeman's night stick would prod him out of his reverie. It was best not to loiter here.

He slowly got to his feet and shuffled along behind the buildings. He poked into boxes and trash bins as he strolled, taking his time as he went but casually glancing around him to make sure he drew no undue attention. He knew he had little to worry about on that account. Few people noticed a homeless man because they wanted to avoid the guilt of seeing someone like him. Eventually most people were able to look right through a street person, as if he were invisible.

Gradually he made his way toward the Island Yacht Club Resort with its stark white stucco buildings topped by Spanish red-tile roofs. The sun had not yet risen too high in the sky. Any later, however, and the staff at the club would be out inspecting the grounds, quickly shooing him away before their guests saw him. He shuffled past the cabanas close to the beach. The smell here was much more pleasant than the odors of the dumpsters on the main street of San Pedro. He could hear Calypso music piped out of speakers near the pool next to the clubhouse about a hundred yards from the beach

He stopped and checked a couple of garbage cans along the walkway. They had been emptied by some conscientious worker already this morning. Ahead he could see the masts of sailboats at the marina.

The berths of the marina were only half full. Five boats of various sizes floated there. One of the boats, a 44-foot Morgan, had not been there when he visited the marina the day before. Maybe there was something of interest there. He paused at the covered pavilion that marked the entrance of the marina and looked around for any of the club employees. No one was stirring.

He walked down the pier slowly, his shopping bag dangling from his fingers. Stopping to poke in the two trash receptacles along the way to the new boat, he let his gaze travel along the wood planks back to the clubhouse. Still no one about.

He stood across from the big sailboat. It was a beauty. He did not look at it directly as he poked through the contents of his bag.

A woman came out on the deck. The homeless man did not seem to notice her. He half-stood and picked up the bag to walk back down the pier.

She was an attractive woman, slim with very short black hair. She stretched and looked out across the water through her sunshades. She glanced at the bum on the pier before turning to go back below.

As she turned, the wind caught the edge of her wrap and blew it briefly aside. She was wearing a black bikini. High on her hip was a mark. It was there then gone. The wrap she was wearing fluttered back to cover her hips.

The bum kept shuffling to the end of the pier.

It had been just a flash. But he had seen it.

The tattoo on the woman's hip.

A tiny red, yellow, and blue butterfly.

# Chapter 33

The red-haired man picked up the Frisbee and walked out onto the island beach. "C'mon, you can do better than that," he called out to the girl. He flicked his wrist and the fluorescent yellow plastic disc floated over to her. She made a half-hearted attempt to catch it but missed. The disc hit the sand, bounced and rolled away on the packed beach all the way to the water's edge.

Jerah Schein rubbed his hand over his newly red hair and watched Hallee walk over to pick up the Frisbee. Her face was as morose as if she had been sentenced to a prison instead of playing on the white sands of a sun-drenched Caribbean isle.

He didn't blame her. Her life had been turned upside down. It would take awhile for her to adjust.

In fact, it would take them all awhile to adjust.

He had been elated during the sail across the Gulf of Mexico into the Caribbean as he steered the new sailboat back toward his beloved island. He should have expected the island to have lost some of its charm in the 15 or so years since he had seen it. But he was still shocked by the number of resorts that occupied the island now.

Maybe this would not be the place he would come to rest after all. Other small islands surrounded Ambergris, undeveloped places he could mold into the perfect hideaway. The less crowded the better.

But this was a good place to rest for a while. So much had happened. He needed the break. He had plenty of time for that now.

He had expected Hallee to adopt a little more cheery attitude when she was reunited with her mother. He was mildly surprised that the girl's sadness had deepened. The tears had flowed from the girl and when they stopped, they were replaced with a questioning look that Hallee would not express in front of Schein. He had expected the child to bolt; somehow her mother had kept her in line.

He hoped that time would heal her pain.

More worrisome to him at this point was the change he had seen in Freida Lamberth.

She had been affectionate to the point of startling him when he first picked her up at the other sailboat where she had staged her disappearance. He remembered the flush of success on her face as she talked of her plan working out perfectly. Her plan. He had let that one pass.

The kidnapping of Hallee had been the widow's idea, he granted that. But the fake suicide/murder – whatever the police deemed it – of Freida Lamberth on the boat, that had been Schein's scheme. "Why live the rest of your life looking over your shoulder? Make them think you're dead," he had said.

During the boat ride to the island, Freida had grown more distant. He knew it was stressful for her to deal with Hallee as the girl was trying to make sense of all that had happened. Now that they were docked at the marina and safe, he hoped she would regain her spirit.

He watched Hallee walk over to the beach blanket he had spread on the white sand. She flopped down on her stomach and stared out over the water.

Much had changed since he had embarked on his mission to New Orleans. Originally, all he had planned was the justified execution of the abortion butcher Tyson Lamberth. Gradually, the mission had expanded in ways he never would have imagined. It started, ironically, with Dr. Lamberth asking him to do some work around his house. He had felt paranoid about the request, wondering if somehow the doctor knew of his plot.

Then came the real surprise. Freida Lamberth had revealed that she had been his benefactor, the one he had met on the Internet who first put the idea in his head to assassinate an abortion doctor. At first, he had been furious, to have been manipulated like that. But he had calmed down when he heard of her years of abuse at the hands of the doctor. The forced abortions, the affairs her husband had flaunted, the virtual prison her home had become for her. The man had actually murdered her unborn children.

And the biggest shocker: Tyson had never wanted Freida to give birth to Hallee but she had threatened to divorce him. He relented.

The doctor had wanted to kill his own daughter. That realization had made the rest of Freida's plan easier to digest.

Schein picked up the Frisbee and waded out into the surf. The water was cool for a second but he quickly adjusted to it. Above his head seagulls floated in the warm breeze. He took a deep breath of the clean salt air and let it out slowly.

All in all, everything had worked out better than expected. Of course, the bodyguard Forte had caused a little more excitement than he had bargained for but that too was past. He considered the man a worthy adversary who had come up short.

The future was ahead. Sometime the next day, the $25 million in ransom money would be transferred into two other accounts: one in the name of his third identity that had been established for him by the junkie papermaker months ago, and one in the fake identity that

Freida had assumed. After that, the pair would shop for property to build the perfect hideaway.

He felt the sun warming his shoulders as he waded waist-deep in the surf. He dipped the disc into the water and scooped up sea water, then let it trickle over the back of his neck and down his spine.

Maybe he would go snorkeling along the barrier reef a little later.

He felt the healing of the water. There would be more to come.

# Chapter 34

The bum stumbled a bit as he walked north on the beach, away from the town. The sand was uneven and darker here, showing the natural color of the island's soil. The business people had yet to haul in the sparkling white sand that made for the tourist-attracting photos on the covers of brochures. A few bungalows were nestled among palm trees along this stretch, a less developed area than the luxury resorts in San Pedro. Ahead of him a mile or so he could see where the mangrove trees still grew almost all the way up to the water's edge, marking the end of the tourist areas of the island.

He had walked away from the yacht club and continued his search for discarded treasures in the back alleys of the town. Crisscrossing from the Caribbean side of town over to the San Pedro Lagoon that bordered the town on the west just a few hundred yards away, he had sorted through dozens of trash cans, all the while slowly making his way northward. He shuffled back and forth, up Buccaneer Street, up across Pescador Drive, down Pelican Street, over to Sandpiper Street and back over to the beach side of town again.

Eventually he had meandered through the park on the north side of town. He had stopped to sit on a bench and patiently sort through the treasures of his morning quest: a ripped pair of jeans, a sodden purple bandana, two right-footed sandals, a pair of sunglasses with the left earpiece missing, and an orange baseball cap with St. Matthew's School of Medicine in bright green letters.

He kept moving north. Using the hand ferry, he crossed the San Pedro River and kept going along the beach. To his right he could see the water taxis scooting along the waves as they carried tourists from the outlying resorts back to the town. The resorts became less extravagant the further he walked. He passed the vacation spots along this stretch of beach: El Pescador, Esseen Way, Captain Morgan's Retreat, Journey's End. These were the less expensive resorts, the ones advertised with sayings like "Experience the simplicity of island life the way it was meant to be."

Now he could see the end of the developed beach area. As he walked slowly around a bend in the sand dunes, he could see the scattering of five small cottages about 80 yards from the beach. He slowed his pace nearly to a standstill as he observed the small clapboard cabins with their fake thatch roofs. None of the cottages seemed to be occupied but there was always the possibility that someone was spying on him behind one of the screenless windows. He waited a moment then resumed his hunched-over stroll toward the buildings.

Without looking up he went from cottage to cottage, lifting the lids to the garbage cans and bending over into them until he was in danger of falling into the battered steel receptacles. Nothing for him here. He stood up and wiped the sweat from his face with the sleeve of his tee-shirt as he leaned against the back of the cottage that was the most secluded of the five.

He swung his head quickly back and forth for any sign of movement. None. He reached over and tried the door knob at the back door of the hut. It turned easily.

He opened the door and went in.

Two single beds bordered the bedroom. A ceiling fan circled lazily overhead. Both windows of the small bedroom were open so that the beach breeze blew through.

A man, scruffy and stained as he, was propped up in one of the beds reading a magazine. He glanced up at the newcomer.

"Any luck?" the man on the bed asked.

"Yes," said the man in the straw hat. He sat on the other bed and took off his hat, then pried the sweaty braided wig off his head. He took out the bandana and wiped his face. "I found her. The mourning widow." He reached down and peeled the sand-caked bandage off his arm. Beneath was a patch of clean skin with the tattoo of a seal.

The other man smiled and his teeth looked white against his dirt-dark skin. "Well, Mr. Forte, you were right," he said.

"Nomad, you doubted me?" said Forte as he peeled off the tee-shirt. The other man chuckled.

"And now," Forte said, " it's time for a swim."

* * *

The grouper sizzled on the grill next to the picnic table behind the cabin. Nomad lifted the edge of the fish steak with a spatula. He quickly flipped it. The sizzling increased. He closed the lid on the grill and sat on the bench seat of the picnic table.

Forte sat on the other side, a legal pad open on the table next to a bottle of root beer.

"So, you saw the mother but neither of the others," Nomad said.

"Right," said Forte. "They have to be nearby, though, I'm sure of it. It would be tough to sail a boat that big without another hand or two."

Nomad nodded and took a swig of his beer. One was his limit. Besides, no need to tempt his friend too much. He enjoyed a brewski on occasion but his loyalty to Forte was stronger than his need to drink.

"You figure they will show up soon," Nomad said.

"Not going to wait on that. We need to move quickly," Forte said. "Tonight."

Nomad grunted his approval and waited for the plan.

# Chapter 35

*Saturday, 9 p.m.*

Tiny white lights dangled from the rafters of the covered pavilion on the marina, giving off what little atmosphere the vacationers at the bar needed in their tropical getaway. The bartender swayed to the four-piece calypso band on the beach as he concocted the fruity drinks for the red-baked people perched on their cane-backed stools.

"It's the little umbrella that gets them," he said to the swarthy man seated in front of him at the bar. "You pop one of those little suckers in a drink and they don't care what else is in there, as long as it tastes sweet and its got some wacky island name like Blue Hawaiian or Tequila Sunrise."

Nomad puffed his cigar and then pointed it at the bartender. "Atmosphere," he said, keeping his eyes on the sailboat near the center of the marina. "People want atmosphere more than anything else."

The bartender smoothed his ponytail, pointed his finger pistol-style at Nomad, and clicked out of the corner of his mouth. "More than anything, pal" he said. "'Cept maybe love." He guffawed at his own joke and moved to take a drink order from two teenage girls.

Nomad, freshly-scrubbed and wearing a flowered shirt and a tan, had been swapping trade talk with the bartender, professing to be a fellow member of the trade, for the past two hours. He had watched a woman and a girl, both in bathing suits, go into the boat at around 7:30 p.m. They had yet to reappear.

The man was nowhere in sight, which was fine with Nomad. Judging from his string of successes in this operation, Schein apparently possessed more than enough skills to make the rescue mission a bloody affair if he had a chance to resist. Though Nomad never backed down from a fight, he would be happy to confront the killer on another day, after the girl was delivered to safety.

He turned and leaned back against the bar as he watched the band. A dozen couples were scattered across the sand on blankets with their drinks. One couple was performing a drunken jitterbug to the music while a group of their friends brayed with laughter and snapped photos. Beyond the band the expanse of beach was dotted with other pavilions with bars and parties of vacationers making the most of their Saturday night on the island. Light flickered on the beach from the flames of Tiki lamps stuck randomly among the dunes behind the yacht club and other resorts.

To his left a movement pulled Nomad's attention around to the boat. A woman with short black hair, wearing a bright sarong, came out of the cabin and stood against the rail. She gazed up at the stars for a moment, then looked up and down the pier. Within a couple of minutes, the girl came out of the cabin, her hair wet. Even from where Nomad sat, he could see clearly that the girl's countenance was unhappy. She stood next to the woman but didn't look up at the sky. The woman put her arm around the girl who merely stood looking down at the water.

Nomad took a sip of his drink, then bent his head as if he were searching his shirt pocket. "The woman and the girl are on deck," he said into the small concealed microphone in his pocket.

"Check," said Forte's voice in his ear piece. "Let's follow the plan. I'll pick them up as they leave the marina. If I can flush out the girl so that she runs for it, you pick her up and get her to a safe place. The police station if you havê to. Remember, whatever happens, stick with the girl."

Nomad knew what his friend was asking him to do. Even if Forte was under threat of death, the girl's welfare must come first. It was the primary goal of the mission and Forte would expect him to accomplish it as planned. He bent his head to the pocket microphone again.

"Check," he said.

* * *

The Barrier Reef looked so different in the night water that Schein wondered if it was the same stretch that he had visited during the afternoon. He gave four strong kicks and his flippers propelled him along the reef until he saw the red ribbon he had tied earlier. This was the spot. He wanted to check out this area of the reef again after dark.

As a boy he had snorkeled along the reef during the summer mission trips. Night snorkeling was off-limits to him back then. Father Buell had always ruled against him on that request. Now, finally he was able to see the reef at night.

Under the brilliance of his underwater light, the coral and sponge were even more vivid against the dark background of the inky water. The shades of orange and pink and blue looked as if some surrealist painter had mixed colors never before used, just for this place. As he glided along, lobsters scurried away from his light. A small octopus stopped its plundering of a crevice and seemed to study him momentarily before shooting away in a cloud of sand. A sea eel swam lazily through the wake of the octopus and began poking its snout in the same crevice abandoned by the eight-legged creature.

In the silence of the sea, Schein felt at peace, more peace than he had experienced in a long while. This reminded him of those peaceful times as a boy when most decisions were made for him and the ones he had to make for himself were of little lasting consequence. No evil here, no disappointments, no embarrassments, no failures. Just beauty suspended below the waves.

He felt so mellow, almost like he wanted to take a nap. He smiled in his scuba mask at the absurdity of that thought. He watched as the underwater flashlight floated away from his hand. So silly, so very silly that he could not hold on to the lamp. Come back, lamp, come on back now.

He watched the bubbles float away from his snorkel mask as he floated, suspended in the water. The current rocked him gently and his face brushed against the razor edges of the reef. He barely felt the sting as the reef sliced his face. The water became tinged with pinkness around his mask now. He raised his arm and raked his fingers slowly through the blood-tinged water. Lovely, so lovely, the pink water and the yellow and blue and orange reef.

His last thought before drifting off was that he should have waited 30 minutes after eating the meal that Freida had prepared for him.

Just for him.

* * *

The music of the islands poured out of the clubs and eateries that lined the beach of San Pedro. To the untrained ear, all the tunes sounded the same with their steel drum melodies overlaid with marimba and the occasional sound of a Mayan harp.

Forte wished he could enjoy the music more but his concentration was on the woman and girl strolling along the beach ahead of him.

The merchants of the island town knew that half of their profit for the week would be made on this night. Most of the shops were still open and it seemed like hundreds of people were out to make the most of their last night on the island.

Forte strolled along behind the pair, allowing other small groups of beach-walkers to block him from being seen by the woman. Not that she would recognize him. He wore a white cap with the words "Belize Rules" in blazing red. His face was half-covered with a full beard, neatly trimmed. He wore glasses and had popped brown-tinted Contacs into his eyes in case he inadvertently got close enough for his face to be recognized.

Some light spilled onto the beach as tourists went in and out of the doors of the restaurants. In the spaces between the eateries, only the flames of the lamps illuminated the sand. Forte was concerned with the visibility here. There was nothing he could do about it. He knew that behind him somewhere Nomad lurked, a fact that comforted him. It would do him no good to try and spot him. It would only frustrate him and take his attention away from those he followed. Nomad had been known to disappear from sight in the middle of a conversation on a town square at midday. He had a gift for concealment.

Ahead of him, Forte saw the woman stop and point to a restaurant. In the dimness of the evening, he could see that the girl did not respond. He wondered if she was drugged.

The woman and girl turned from the beach path and walked along a creaking boardwalk that led to the door of the place. Forte followed them. A small sign with "The Crazy Parrot" on it hung above the door. A stuffed parrot with a pipe in its beak leaned drunkenly on the end of the sign.

Inside, a combo of three musicians was finishing up the last song of a set before the group took a break. Freida and Hallee sat at a table not far from the bar. Forte walked past them to the bar and ordered a coke and an appetizer of crab cakes. He sat sideways on the stool and listened to the fading notes of the band.

As he turned back to the bar he locked eyes with Freida briefly. Was she looking at him? Her face showed no recognition. He turned around and sipped his coke.

The room seemed nearly silent as the musicians made their way to the far end of the bar. Forte turned his head slightly. He could catch snatches of conversation from Freida's table.

" ... it's a shop I saw earlier. It's just next door. I'll be right back," Freida's voice floated over to him.

He watched in the mirror behind the bar as she got up and went out the front door of the restaurant.

Forte counted to ten slowly then got up and walked over to the table. Hallee sat with her head propped in her hands, her elbows on the table as she stared into a blue-colored drink. He leaned over, his hands resting on the table. The jukebox cranked up, banishing the silence from the room.

"Do not act surprised. Just look at me and smile," he said.

The girl did not respond at first. Her head lifted and Forte watched the series of emotions travel across her features. Annoyance first, at having a stranger approach her table. Then puzzlement. Then the raising of her eyebrows in surprise, followed by relief mixed with fear.

Forte put a finger to his lips. "This may be confusing for you, so I am asking you to trust me. I want you to get up and go out that back door as quickly as you can. Just keep walking. A man in a flower shirt will meet you there. His name is Nomad." He paused. "You are safe now, Hallee."

Forte watched her face as her eyes began to film with tears. Then another cloud of fear gripped her face. She was looking behind him.

He could feel the heat of another person's body close against his back. Then he felt the gun.

The voice of Freida Lamberth whispered in his ear. "Yes, she is safe now." Everything in the room seemed dulled now as the pistol bore into his back, the colors drained, the sound muted. "She is safe. But you aren't."

Forte looked at Hallee. The girl's eyes darted back and forth between his face and her mother's.

Hallee stood up and took a small step away from the table.

"Hallee," her mother said in a low tone, "sit down. Now."

Hallee took another step backwards.

Freida hissed at her now, biting off each word. "Hallee... you'd... better..."

The girl walked away from the table quickly.

Forte watched as Hallee opened the back door of The Crazy Parrot. She looked back, her face a mask of sadness. She went out into the darkness.

# Chapter 36

*Saturday, 10:00 p.m.*

The inside of the boat was bigger than Forte had imagined it would be. He sat in a lounge chair facing the cold fury of Freida Lamberth.

"You know that all of this was for nothing, your little 'rescue trip' down here." She spat the words at him. With her new black hair cut so severely, her green eyes seemed harder. Were it possible, those eyes would cut into him like pinpoints of laser.

"In the morning, you will be at the bottom of the gulf and the crabs will be picking at your flesh," she said. The nine-millimeter automatic was steady in her hand. It was pointed at his head.

Forte remained silent. He sat in the chair with his hands on top of his head, his fingers intertwined. She could not figure out how to bind his hands and legs without putting down the gun. Forte had no doubt, however, that she would shoot him. He could see no sign of shakiness in the hand that held the pistol.

Freida cursed. "If you only knew…"

"If I knew what?" he said.

She glared at him, her lips pressed together in a hard line. "It was almost over. The perfect ending," she said.

"You planned it all, didn't you?"

She blinked. "Not this. I didn't plan this."

"This?"

"I... didn't plan... to have to kill you." Her words came out slowly, but without regret.

"But everything else..."

Freida's mouth turned up into a mirthless smile. "Yes. I did. I planned it all."

She waved the gun. "Get up slowly and walk ahead of me."

They climbed the stairs out of the cabin. Freida motioned for him to stand on the deck area forward of the cabin. Forte backed up until he was against the guard rail along the bow.

"Where is Jerah Schein?" he said.

"That fool. He thought he was helping me. He deserved to die for his stupidity alone." Freida laughed and the sound of it made Forte think of the cackling of a demented woman.

"You killed him?" he asked.

The woman nodded. "Right about now, the crabs should be nibbling at him. He deserved it. He thought he would have me but you got closer to that than he did." She laughed again and Forte forced himself to look at her face as it twisted with evil. "I was good, wasn't I, Mr. Forte? When you were in my bedroom with me, you forgot about poor little Hallee for a few minutes, didn't you?"

She pulled back the hammer on the automatic. The click sounded deadly.

If he could keep her talking, there might be a chance. "And your husband, the father of your child, what about him?" he asked. "He deserved to die too?"

Freida smiled more broadly now. "Oh yes. Many people thought so. We got hate mail about it all the time. People would have stood in line to kill him." Her smile faded. "But I was the lucky one. He killed three of my babies before they ever had a chance. And he wanted to kill Hallee, too, before she ever saw the light of day. But I stopped him. I stopped him."

Her face was steel now. "And at the end, he had the gall to give most of his money to everyone else but me. After all I did, putting him through medical school, giving him a beautiful home, keeping quiet during all of his nasty little affairs." Her voice cracked. "The bastard deserved it a million times over."

Suddenly, a voice spoke from the other side of the bow. "Yes, he did."

Freida whirled, her arm straight with the gun at shoulder level.

Everything happened at once.

Jerah Schein was standing next to the rail along the bow opposite him. The right side of his face dribbled blood from three gashes. The blood had run down his face, his neck and into his chest hair.

At the sound of his voice, Freida spun toward him and shot him.

His face jerked sideways as the bullet hit him. A spurt of blood came out of his left eye. He tumbled backward over the rail.

Forte's foot lashed out and Freida's legs buckled. She slammed down on the deck and bounced once like a rag doll. She lay still.

Forte scrambled to pick up the pistol which had clattered across the deck.

He ran to the edge of the dented rail where Schein had gone over. He pointed the pistol down at the water abeam the sailboat.

The man was gone.

Freida groaned and Forte stepped close to her. He took a pair of handcuffs out of his back pocket and clicked them over her wrists.

In the other boats along the marina, people were coming out of their cabins. In the muted lights of the boats, their faces looked worried — but curious. Forte got to his feet and waved at the onlookers. "Everything's under control," he called out.

The deck of the boat rolled gently under his feet, a rocking motion, soothing in its contrast to the burst of violence. Forte looked up at the masts of the other sailboats docked nearby, their flags atop fluttering in the island breeze. Beyond them a navy sky dappled with specks of light.

He looked down at the unconscious woman then slowly slid down to the deck and sat with his back against the cabin of the boat.

It was over.

He reached into his pocket again and pulled out a tiny digital recorder. He clicked it off.

# Chapter 37

*A few days later.*

"Go fastuh, Unka Alvey! Go fastuh!" the curly-haired toddler squealed as she clung to Forte's ears. He scooted across the Quadries' back yard on all fours until he finally mock-collapsed in a heap.

"This old horse needs a break, Katie Quadrie," he told the girl. He lay flat on his back in the grass. She crawled up on his chest so that her aqua eyes looked directly into his yellow eyes. Katie wrinkled her nose and put her finger on the tip of his nose. "I need a new horsey," she announced. She jumped up and ran over to Archie Griffey who sat at a picnic table chatting with Manny Laird. The retired cop scooped her up and put her on his back and scampered across the yard.

"Dinner is served!" Mack Quadrie called out as he finished flipping the burgers off the grill onto a huge platter. His wife Renee came out of the house with an oversized serving bowl filled with baked beans and set it on the picnic table next to the grill. Jackie Shaw followed with another giant bowl, this one full of potato salad.

"Manny, why don't you bless our food," Mack said to the pastor. After the prayer, everyone milled around the table filling plates for a few moments until they got settled.

"So, they haven't recovered Schein's body yet?" Mack asked abruptly.

Renee elbowed him in the ribs. "Mack, honey, what kind of dinner conversation is that!"

Her giant of a husband bit off a third of his hamburger and looked at Forte.

Forte drank his root beer and set the bottle next to his plate. "Not yet. They likely never will. It's my understanding that the little sea scavengers can do their work pretty quickly." He waggled his eyebrows at Katie who giggled at him.

"What about the rest of it?" asked Archie. "The girl and her mother."

"Freida Lamberth is awaiting trial without bond. Her lawyers were unable to convince the judge she was not a flight risk after everything that happened. And Hallee is at her grandparents' house trying to make sense of her life," Forte said.

"Poor girl," said Manny.

"Yeah, it's going to take some time for her to get over it, not that she will ever be able to put it out of her mind," Forte said. "Her mother told her that her father had wanted to have her aborted. A child shouldn't have to deal with that kind of hard truth."

"No," said Jackie Shaw. "None of us should have to."

Everyone ate in silence for a few minutes under the bright April sky. Finally Verna Griffey spoke up. "The ransom money. Did they get it back?" She looked around the table. "Y'all know you want to find out about that." Everyone laughed.

Forte finished chewing and swallowed. "The last I heard, the FBI and CIA both were trying to track down the twenty-five million.

They followed the trail to two other bank accounts in Switzerland and Hong Kong before they lost it. The money is gone."

Verna set down her glass of iced tea. "Whole lotta money to just go poof," she said.

"But the girl is safe," Forte said.

"Amen," said Manny Laird.

The conversation traveled in other directions, to Mack's exploits as a star defensive tackle for the Saints, Archie's latest fishing tales, and Katie's outstanding accomplishments in kindergarten. Everyone helped clear the table and Renee went in the house with Verna to put on coffee. Mack took Archie to show him a new fishing lure he had picked up. Jackie took Katie's hand and walked across the backyard to a sandbox.

Forte and Manny walked around the back yard under the pecan trees, letting the meal settle a bit before the banana pudding was brought out.

"You did a good thing, you and Nomad," Manny said. His blue eyes were the color of the Caribbean.

"We did what we had to do," Forte said.

"Yes. Most men would not have been able to do it."

Forte stooped and picked up one of Katie's pink shoes from the lawn. "It's what I know to do," he said. "I don't give myself another choice."

Manny considered that. "Everyone has choices. You've made bad ones before, as we all have. You made a good choice this time. Accept that," he said.

Forte looked down at his friend's weathered face and saw the kindness there.

"Okay," he said.

"Okay," Manny said.

\* \* \*

The woman stood in the hallway and watched her two daughters: one wanting to be so grown-up and the other just beginning her life.

Joyce smiled as she saw how lovingly Angie held the baby. Her eldest daughter looked older than her thirteen years as she cradled the newborn on the sofa. Somehow the girl's icy emotional surface had melted a bit since Joyce came home from the hospital. The thaw had surprised both of them.

At first, after the incident, she had wondered how she could survive it. Seeing the doctor murdered had rocked her. Her world was turned upside down with all of the police's questions and the investigation. And … the baby.

Then, they brought the tiny bundle into her room. Little Sarah. She held the premature child in her arms and looked into that little face. Her worries had faded away. Her life had changed.

It would not be easy. But it was her life.

We are a mixed-up fruit salad of a family, she thought as she watched her two daughters cuddle on the sofa. But we are here. Together.

# *Epilogue*

*Some time later.*

The late afternoon sun warmed the deck of the sailboat as it raced across the waves.

The man at the wheel watched the clouds building on the horizon and decided it was time to turn back toward the Australian coastline. Soon the sun would disappear and the winter winds of the southern hemisphere would make it too cold to stay out on the water for very long.

He rubbed a hand over his shaved head, then reached to adjust the black patch over his left eye. The blond beard he was growing just barely concealed the trio of scars that raked across his right cheek. He could feel the ridges of the scars as his fingers probed beneath the beard.

There would be time to heal. And money to make the healing as comfortable as it could be.

No need to plan too far ahead. Yet.

**The End**

## *About the Author*

Glen Allison and his wife Kathy live in northeast Mississippi. He is co-founder of the Mississippi Writers Club and is the author of <u>Still Standing Tall</u>, the story of the Williams Brothers, by Billboard Books. He has written for MISSISSIPPI magazine, MEMPHIS magazine, MISSISSIPPI BUSINESS JOURNAL, and others. MISCUE is the first in the Al Forte mystery-suspense series from Yoke Press. Glen can be reached by e-mail at glen@netga.com.

For more information about MISCUE, go to:

# Yokepress.com

*Coming Soon from Yoke Press!*

# NETBLUE

The second in the Al Forte mystery series

Just when you thought things would settle down for Al Forte, the New Orleans bodyguard finds himself on the hunt for an Internet assassin. The targets of the murderer? Pedophiles who have been released from prison. Ordinarily, Forte wouldn't spend a minute's worry on the serial killer's spree, but his attention is captured when a child is threatened.

Glen Allison's new novel once again plunges Al Forte into a situation that challenges his sense of right and wrong and threatens his own mission in life.

For a sample of **NETBLUE**,

*keep reading....*

## *An excerpt from* **NETBLUE**

Copyright © 2002 by Glen Allison

Perspiration trickled down the middle of Al Forte's back under the Kevlar vest as he crouched in the cave-black hallway. Inside the abandoned building, the heat sweltered even more than the 98-degree east Texas afternoon outside. Forte held the H&K sub-machine-gun with one hand and pushed the night-vision goggles up with the other hand as he wiped the sting of sweat from his eyes. Without the goggles he literally could not see his hand in front of his face.

The heat and the darkness annoyed Forte but did nothing serious to crack his resolve.

The baby must be found.

He flipped down the goggles. Behind him were the other two members of the Forte Security rescue team, Nomad Jones and Jackie Shaw. He motioned them to follow as he moved silently down the hallway. Pieces of torn wallboard dotted the floor as they advanced toward the corridor tee-junction ahead. A quick peek around the corner showed no hint of light in either direction. At the far end of the hall to the right was a stairwell.

The faint hum of a radio was drifting down the stairs.

As the team slowly moved toward the stairwell, Forte reminded himself of the details of this mission he had memorized: A escaped convicts had stolen nine-month-old boy from a judge's home the day before. Negotiations had yielded nothing because the kidnappers refused to talk. They had made no ransom demands. They simply wanted revenge against the man who had put them behind bars. Two of the thugs had performed the actual kidnapping but another suspect had driven the getaway car. A strategic and forceful rescue attempt was the only hope for recovery of the child. The team had to be prepared for resistance from at least three men armed with shotguns.

The judge had insisted on using Forte Security for the rescue attempt because this type of mission was the sole reason for the company's existence: recovering and protecting children in danger. Not rich executives held hostage by money-hungry fiends, not diplomats plucked from embassies by terrorists. Just children who found themselves in hostile hands with little hope of a future. To save them was Forte's life, one of the few reasons for living he had grasped during the past few years.

He motioned for the others to follow. The journey of 20 feet down the hallway took a full minute as the trio stepped through the debris of the old building with their rubber-soled boots. A tiny sound from a kicked piece of plaster could cause the kidnappers to open fire. At the bottom of the stairwell Forte signaled the other two to stop. The stairs were concrete and steel. Hopefully they would not creak. He tested the first two steps with his half-weight. They were silent. He flipped off the safety on his machine gun and slowly walked up the first flight of stairs. At the first landing he waited. He could hear the radio more clearly now. Above him, the faintest bit of light touched the wall next to the second floor hallway. If there was a sentry, he would be there.

After his team joined him on the landing, he signaled for Nomad to go high and Jackie low after he checked for the sentry. Easing his face to the corner, he took a deep breath and looked quickly. A husky man in a dirty sweatshirt and camouflage pants was leaning next to a door that was cracked open to spill light into the hallway. He ducked back and held up one finger: One guard. He slowly stepped around the corner. The man's head had bobbed down as he fought sleep. Forte noiselessly covered the eight steps that separated them, clamped a hand over the man's mouth and drew his special knife across his throat. Forte held the guard, lowering him to the floor without a sound.

He listened. No stirring came out of the room. The radio droned on. He waved the other two toward him. All three flipped off the night-vision goggles now that light was available.

From his belt Forte took a tiny electronic periscope with a flexible wand tipped with a lens the size of a pencil eraser. He bent the wand carefully and put the viewfinder to his eye. He repositioned the periscope twice along the edge of the doorway and repeated the process to get a full picture of the room. He extracted the wand from the doorway. He felt the others' eyes on him.

He rocked his arms over his chest to indicate the child was there, then pointed to the left side of the room. Then he crossed his arms, held up two fingers, then pointed once to the center of the room and once to the right side: There were two other people in the room. He signaled again to remind them of the order of attack. They would enter on the count of three.

Forte watched as Nomad pulled a flash grenade from his belt. To his left, Jackie was crouched, her mouth grim but eyes calm.

He held up one finger. One.

Two fingers.

A commercial for cellphone service blared on the radio inside the room.

Three fingers.

Nomad lobbed the flash grenade into the room, tossing it high to give it time to explode before hitting the floor. The blast of the grenade was timed exactly with the crash of the door as Nomad burst into the room. He rolled on to the floor and shot the man on the right with a two quick blasts before the kidnapper could move. Forte could see the man's mouth formed a surprised "O" as he flew backwards.

Jackie followed immediately and put three bullets into the middle of the chest of the man half-standing in the center of the room. The kidnapper had kicked his chair backward, leaped up from his chair at a chipped kitchen table and was grabbing for a shotgun when the rounds from Jackie's weapon knocked him backwards.

A baby's scream punctuated the gunfire.

Forte sprinted to the left corner and flung his body over the small cardboard box holding the child. Smoke from the flash-bang grenade drifted waist-high throughout the room.

"Target One down and out," Nomad shouted.

Jackie immediately called out. "Target Two down and out."

Forte rolled away from the box and looked inside it. He reached down to pull out the baby cocooned in its bundle of blankets.

It was a plastic doll. Forte kissed the toy on its forehead and placed it back in the box.

A loudspeaker blared somewhere above the room. "Exercise concluded! Well done, Team Forte." A man in fatigues carrying a clipboard stepped into the room from the hallway. "Strategy... Excellent... Execution... Excellent... Response time...excellent. Your scores keep getting better and better, Al." Forte lifted a hand to give a weak wave in response. Even though the rescue had been a simulation his adrenaline had spiked and was now draining, just as if the mission had been real. The men who had played the part of the kidnappers got up from floor and patted him on the shoulder as they left the room.

Twice a year, Forte spent a couple of days at the Firestorm Training Center in the Big Thicket area of Texas just across the

Louisiana border. Mike "Nomad" Jones came along for at least one of the training sessions each year. Nomad, whose nickname came from his response of "No Matter" back in his days with Forte as Navy SEALS, was leaning over with his hands on his knees, his head below the haze in the room.

This was the first time at the training center for Jackie Shaw, the thirty-something resident director of The Refuge, a shelter for endangered children that Forte had established. She had been hired a year earlier and had already experienced an attack on the shelter. An expert marksman, she had brought down one of the attackers with a shot to the leg. She deserved the extra training. Forte still smiled when he recalled she was an ex-nun.

"Quite a buzz, huh?" Forte asked.

Jackie was sitting at the table running a hand over the white streak in her closely-cropped black hair. She lifted her head. "Yeah. My ears are still ringing from the flash-bang." She tossed a set of earplugs on the table. "Even with these things plugged in."

"Good job," Forte said. "Both of you." He pulled out a slightly dented pack of Checkers cigarettes from a zippered pocked on his fatigues. He was down to four smokes a day. The Checkers were nasty but they were all that was left of more troubled times. He shook out Number Three and lit it up.

Nomad straightened up, his eyes white against the black-and-green streaks of camo paint on his face. "In the words of the Indian chief to John Wayne in McClintock, 'Good party, no mo' whiskey, we go home.'"

All three people in the room laughed. They began taking off the special sensor weapons provided by the training center and stacking them on the table in the center of the room.

The whump-whump of helicopter blades penetrated the thin walls of the tattered building.

"Must be another simulation exercise," said Nomad.

The whirring of the chopper blades slowed as the craft landed outside. Suddenly, a voice came over the speakers. "Al Forte, you have company outside."

Forte took off his gun belt and vest and handed them to Nomad before retracing his steps down the stairs and out of the building. A sleek blue corporate helicopter rested in an open area 50 yards away. A man in a business suit was walking toward him bent over as the blades whirled at half-speed.

The man extended his hand as he approached. "Mr. Forte? I'm Thomas Penderby with VillaCom, the telecommunications company. May we step inside for a moment?"

Away from the noise, Penderby came straight to the point. "Mr. Bryce Graham needs your help. His daughter is missing. She's 14 and Mr. Bryce wants the best help available. That's why I'm here."

Forte studied the man. He knew of the company because it was in New Orleans, not far from The Refuge. Penderby's brow was creased as he stood stoop-shouldered in the dusty foyer of the building. His boss was a man who exerted a lot of pressure.

"Has she been kidnapped?" Forte asked.

"We think so, yes."

"But, no ransom demands have been made?"

The man looked down. His collar above the pink silk tie was stained with sweat. "No, not yet."

"So, she could be a runaway," Forte said.

Penderby looked up. "Please. Mr. Bryce just wants his daughter safe at home again." The man looked on the verge of tears. "He said to tell you Mrs. Christenberry recommended you."

That explained how the man had tracked him down. Ordinarily his office would not have released information on his whereabouts. Verna Griffey, his assistant, would have responded to the Christenberry name, however. Forte had recovered Mrs. Christenberry's grandson from kidnappers in Italy four years earlier. It had been his first major case after opening the security firm. The Christenberrys, leaders in New Orleans social and political circles, had donated a large sum of money to make The Refuge a reality. Besides that, Louise Christenberry was his bridge partner.

"When was she last seen?" Forte asked.

"This morning, when Mr. Graham went to work," Penderby said.

"How old is she?"

"About to turn 15."

"So, she's not driving yet."

"Right. Well, she doesn't have her own car yet."

"How do you know she isn't at a friend's house," Forte said.

Penderby looked embarrassed. "Well, she was sort of, um, grounded."

Forte sighed.

"But there's evidence she went to meet someone from a chat group she had been visiting," Penderby said. "We think she is in danger."

"She met someone from the net."

"Right. We found some notes she'd left on her computer."

Forte gazed across the clearing where the helicopter sat. Beyond the aircraft, a hawk circled lazily in the sky. He wondered if the bird had a victim in view or was just biding his time in the hot August sky until something turned up. He turned back to Penderby.

"When does Mr. Graham want to meet with me?"

"As soon as you can do it," the man said. "He will be at his house, waiting for you. The chopper can have us there in an hour." The man's face was flushed now.

"Let me tell my crew," Forte said. "But you need to know that I'm not agreeing to find the girl yet. I'll meet with Graham and then we'll see."

Penderby grabbed his hand. He had done what he could do. "Fine, fine, Mr. Forte, that's all we ask."

"Sure," Forte said. "That's what they all say."

⌘　⌘　⌘　⌘　⌘

*For more information on NETBLUE, stay tuned to*

Yokepress.com